SURRENDER
to SIN

THE FALLEN SERIES

Happy reading!

Nicole.

SURRENDER *to* SIN

THE FALLEN SERIES

nicola davidson

This book is a work of fiction. Names, characters, places, and incidents are the product of the author's imagination or are used fictitiously. Any resemblance to actual events, locales, or persons, living or dead, is coincidental.

Copyright © 2016 by Nicola Davidson. All rights reserved, including the right to reproduce, distribute, or transmit in any form or by any means. For information regarding subsidiary rights, please contact the Publisher.

Entangled Publishing, LLC
2614 South Timberline Road
Suite 109
Fort Collins, CO 80525
Visit our website at www.entangledpublishing.com.

Scorched is an imprint of Entangled Publishing, LLC.

Edited by Kate Brauning
Cover design by Erin Dameron-Hill
Cover art from Period Images

Manufactured in the United States of America

First Edition December 2016

entangled
scorched

*As always, for Sherilee Gray, CP and friend extraordinaire.
Also, to those striving to make the world a better, kinder, safer
place for all: thank you.*

Chapter One

Gloucester, England, May 1814

"Ah, there you are, Grace. Lord Baxter and I have been waiting."

Lady Grace Carrington somehow kept her smile in place as she curtsied. Anyone would think she had been lazing on a chaise eating sweets, not distributing food baskets to the poor within her father's parish. This was typical from Bishop Lord Harold Lloyd-Gates, though. Even twenty-three years after her birth, he'd never forgiven her for being a daughter rather than the longed-for son.

"I apologize, Father," she replied politely, starting to perspire. Though it was spring, he always kept his library at furnace temperature. "And to you, Lord Baxter. I wasn't aware you were paying a call today, my goodness, I haven't seen you since Carrington's funeral. How are you keeping?"

Lord Baxter smiled but there was no kindness or joy in it. Was the man even capable of such emotions? Forty years her senior, the same age as her father and her late husband the Earl Carrington, yet so much colder. Infinitely stuffier. And the way his deadened, pale blue eyes stared on the few occasions they'd spoken made her skin crawl. "Well enough, Lady Carrington. I merely came here to inspect you and sign the contracts. Pleasingly, all is ready for June first."

All the air whooshed from her lungs. *Inspect? Contracts?* "Excuse me?"

"One always makes a last inspection before purchase, even knowing the beauty and bloodlines. Despite your failure to give Carrington an heir, your family physician assures me there is no impediment. I must say, though, gowns revealing bare arms and collarbone like the one you wear are neither appropriate nor good for your health, and will be burned and replaced in London. Lady Baxter will not dress like a strumpet."

Horror enveloped Grace, dark and suffocating, and her fists clenched in the folds of her lavender day dress. No. Surely her father couldn't be so cruel again. She'd paid her blasted filial dues: five interminable, loveless and passionless years as Countess Carrington, until the earl blessedly made her a widow. His delighted nephew hadn't even needed to chase her out the estate door once the inheritance legalities were settled. And on returning home, her father and stepmother had sworn she could either embrace widowhood or remarry as she pleased.

Oh, the wicked daydreams she'd had of finding a gentleman like the one who'd fueled a thousand secret fantasies. She'd only seen him once, six years ago in Hyde Park, but the memory had been seared forever in her mind. Young. All-conquering. Broad shoulders, muscled thighs, dark-haired and gloriously handsome, with a wicked grin that spoke of unimaginable pleasures.

She'd wager a man like that wouldn't follow a twice-weekly routine: A quarter hour, fully clothed in a darkened, silent bedchamber, hurting his lover's unready body because female pleasure was irrelevant and in fact, immoral. No, he would kiss and touch and stroke. Prepare his woman so thoroughly she'd beg him to take her, and he would, whenever and wherever she wanted. Rough or gentle, fast or slow, not content until she came apart in his arms several times.

Indeed, as her forced year of mourning came to a close, the chance of sexual freedom had beckoned seductively as a siren. And now it was being torn away from her.

"No, Father!" Grace burst out, too shocked, too furious to temper her voice to the quiet, decorous level he required in conversation. "You promised. You said I could remain a widow or choose my own husband!"

"What an unseemly display from your daughter, my lord bishop," said Lord Baxter, his lips thinning further in distaste. "Surely she understands the enormous honor of my name, address, wealth, and position."

"Yes, my lord!" her father said, gripping her arm and dragging her toward the door. "Of course she does. Grace is merely overwhelmed with delight. Perhaps you might excuse us for a moment?"

Lord Baxter nodded approvingly. "By all means. In situations such as these, correction is most appropriate. I commend your values."

Alone in the narrow hallway, Grace wrenched from her father's hand. "No. Not ever. He's far worse than Carrington. Besides, I'm well past my majority, and have a widow's jointure. You cannot force this."

"On the contrary," he hissed, anger reddening his face. "The new earl sent word yesterday. He visited the property set aside for your income, and it's in a terrible state of neglect. Crumbling manor, unploughed and badly watered fields…it will take years to put right. No one was expecting the old earl to pass when he did."

"But I still have money, don't I? What about the

inheritance from Mama?"

"You cannot touch that until you are twenty-five. And I cannot keep you until then, you know very well I have next to nothing of my own. Everything belongs to Waverly, and your uncle near-strangles me with his purse strings."

Despair and fury threatened to choke her at the bald-faced lie. No clergyman in the world lived as well as her father did. His older brother, the Duke of Waverly, had always been fair and obliging.

"Perhaps if I spoke with His Grace—"

"I already have," her father cut in smoothly. "Waverly agrees with me. Baxter is an excellent choice. You often lament your lack of children; his lordship is still healthy and would no doubt give you several."

Her stomach roiled. Yes, she'd always wanted babies to lavish affection on. Yet to become pregnant, to have another soft-bellied, sour-breathed ancient regularly lift her nightgown and dispassionately force himself inside her until he climaxed, could not be tolerated. "But…"

"There is no 'but,' Grace. You will marry Lord Baxter on June first, which will allow your mourning period to come to an end, and a new, more fitting wardrobe to be created. My word, I cannot believe what a disobedient, disloyal daughter you've become. If your mother could see you now, she'd be so sad. So ashamed."

Reeling at the words, Grace staggered backward. "Mama loved me."

"Foolishly," he conceded with a shrug. "But that is the past. The future is us dining with Baxter at six o'clock sharp to celebrate."

Unable to be around him a moment longer, Grace fled the manse for the orchard, her favorite spot for privacy. Underneath a tree groaning with the weight of shiny red apples, she picked up several and hurled them at the massive trunk, unable to hit the blasted thing because her vision was too blurred by hot tears.

She'd been so close. Mere weeks away from re-entering society as a widow and enjoying the associated freedoms like embarking on a discreet but lusty affair. Her dream man would be long-married, but London was the largest of cities. She could have discovered the joys of a young, handsome, and caring lover, a man chosen by her and her alone. Now, yet again, her father had sold her to an ancient who wanted a mute, pretty doll to trot out at balls, soirees, and political dinners, while isolating her in the country for the rest of the year.

"Lady C! What happened? Why are you crying?"

Grace looked over to see the plump form of Nell, her beloved maid-companion, hurrying toward her. Carrington had permitted her employment because she was the spinster sister of a well-bred baronet, and luckily Nell always remembered to mind her naughty tongue around him.

"The worst possible news, Nell."

The silver-haired woman shot her an alarmed look as she collapsed in a heap of starched, gray-striped cambric. "*No.* He wouldn't dare."

"I'm to marry Lord Baxter on June first."

"Argh," spat Nell. "A raging pox on both their hides. What are you going to do?"

"Do? I have very little money. No home of my own. I don't have a choice in this."

"Unless old Baxter cried off for some reason."

"I very much doubt he would."

"He might. If you forced his hand."

Grace stilled, a tiny sliver of hope straightening her shoulders. "His lordship is far stuffier than Carrington ever was. What if…what if I were involved in some sort of scandal?"

"Oooh, yes. Wouldn't take much for his uppity head to explode."

"Baxter is a prude, and believes he is a catch beyond all," said Grace slowly, mentally sifting and discarding ideas. "I think...I think my scandal must be with a man. No, not just a man, an utterly wicked, utterly charming rake with a head for intrigue."

"You need Sin," said Nell sagely.

Laughter bubbled up inside her. "Sin in general or one sin in particular?"

"Oh my poor pet," continued Nell, her eyes gleaming. "You've been buried in the country far too long. The thoroughly scrumptious Lord Sebastian St. John; everyone knows him as Sin. His late mama was a retired courtesan. He keeps not one mistress but an entire harem, and has been at the heart of several jaw-dropping scandals. Yet he's most notorious for part-owning Fallen."

"*Fallen*?" she repeated in confusion. "Is that a racehorse?"

Nell giggled like a debutante. "Good heavens no, although the amount of riding that probably gets done there... Fallen is a private pleasure club that opened about four years ago, caters to *everything* sexual, and is so exclusive that only the richest, highest ranking people in England can apply for membership. All the stuffed shirts like my brother are forever crusading to get it shut down and the three owners banished, but another rumor has the Prince of Wales himself as a patron, so it stays."

"Well," said Grace, her heart lifting by the moment. "This Sin sounds like just the man I need. And I've got an excuse to go to London, since Lord Baxter strongly disapproves of my current strumpet wardrobe."

Nell snorted. "Good grief. The mourning sacks you wear are practically nun's habits. But new gown fittings take forever to do properly. Measurements, fashion plates, trims and fabrics...a fortnight at least."

Their eyes met in perfect understanding. Two whole

weeks to hopefully secure Sin's assistance, then create enough of a scandal that Lord Baxter would run screaming in the other direction. If she could just get rid of him, surely there was some way to petition the courts for earlier access to her mother's money.

But one thing was certain. Under no circumstances would she be a forced bride again.

• • •

London

No one ever wanted to leave Fallen.

Leaning against a cream silk-covered wall, Lord Sebastian St. John, fifth Baron St. John but known to all as Sin, smiled and nodded at the masked procession of England's elite trudging reluctantly out the club's oak double doors. Dawn always heralded the end of a night's revelry, the cool, bleak light a harsh reminder that the club was only a temporary respite, but at least their members didn't have far to go. Fallen was an enormous three-story, red brick townhouse located in fashionable Portman Square, neighbor to several dukes, and a short carriage ride from Hyde Park, Carlton House, Whitehall, and Westminster.

And they would be back, these leading aristocrats of the *ton*, for nowhere else in London could their specific sexual needs be met so well—and so lavishly. A quick fuck in a darkened corner with a bored lover for hire wouldn't do. These men and women wanted the very best money could buy—a decadent sanctuary of champagne, brandy, French chef-prepared delicacies, attentive servants, palatial surroundings, no judgement, and above all, absolute discretion. If a lady wished to be plundered by two men simultaneously, she could. If a gentleman desired to be bound and whipped by his "governess," he was welcome. If married couples decided to swap spouses for the evening, or simply watch others act out a pirate ship or harem orgy fantasy, Fallen was the place.

No request was too much trouble, and for that, membership was strictly monitored, obscenely expensive, and bound by an ironclad contract.

"I say, Sin, jolly good show tonight. Something about a woman between another woman's thighs that stirs the juices, what? Wonder if Maria could be persuaded. I'd dearly love to watch another lady pleasure her while she took me in her mouth."

Sin bowed, somehow managing not to strangle the Prince Regent who had yet again broken one of Fallen's cardinal rules and taken off his club-issued black and white satin demi mask before leaving. Anonymity was critical here; not only did it allow the freedom to fully indulge, but it halted the threat of blackmail. Each mask was individually tailored and numbered; only Sin, and his co-owners Devil and Vice, knew the society leader behind it.

"Should Your Royal Highness and Mrs. Fitzherbert wish it, most anything can be arranged."

The Prince Regent beamed like a toddler given a favorite sweet. Amazing how much their future monarch resembled one, too, with his elaborately embroidered clothing, rumpled hair, and florid, fleshy jowls. "Lovely. How marvelous this club is. No lowborn riff-raff. Can't stand them, or the virtue brigade always hounding me. Spending! Women! Drinking! Bah. They will be sorry for scolding me when I hold a different rank. Mark my words, they will."

Ignoring the petulant tone, Sin smiled easily. "Quite. I shall look forward to your company again soon, sir."

"Right you are. Give my best to Devil, naughty man, staying in his office to count guineas when he could be drinking with me. Even Vice took time from his busy evening to have a brandy."

"Poor form. I shall take him to task at once."

Prinny trotted happily away, and Sin rolled his eyes as he strolled to the suite of offices on the second floor. It was ridiculous to feel so damned irritable and restless when life was practically perfect.

He part-owned the most exclusive pleasure club in England. Held more wealth than could be spent in ten lifetimes. Enjoyed robust good health, the friendship of the highest ranking men in the land, and an incomparable selection of stunningly beautiful, exquisitely hedonistic women who eagerly shared his bed.

Suppressing his temper, Sin unlocked the office door and kicked it shut behind him.

"Prinny has you in his sights again, Devil. Would it kill you to have a drink with the man once in a while, just to shut him up?"

Lord Grayson Deveraux sat back in his chair and ran impatient, ink-covered fingertips through his short-cropped black hair. "Yes. The punishment for poisoning a prince is death, and I wouldn't be able to help myself once he started whining about debts and the sheer unfairness of his life. Honestly don't know why we allow him membership. He's three payments behind now."

"Because he's the future King of England," said an amused, lilting voice. Sin glanced over his shoulder to where Iain, Viscount Vissen, nicknamed Vice, was loosening his cravat. How the red-haired Scot remained immaculate when he spent his evenings managing every aspect of the club's activities—and often joining in—was a minor miracle.

"Wouldn't have thought that carried much weight with you," replied Devil.

Vice shrugged. "The secret to success is keeping friends close and enemies closer. Besides, if you want to talk missing income, ask Sin here why we have another three new parlor maids taking elocution lessons to remove their East End twang. He won't stop until he's rescued every unhappy lightskirt in London, you know. Either that or he's murdered in his bed by a disgruntled abbess."

Pouring two fingers of premium brandy, Sin then raised his glass in a salute. "Dancing with such danger adds a little excitement to my day. Besides, they are hard workers, very loyal."

"And somewhat remind you of your mother," said Devil quietly, stacking leather-bound ledgers into a neat pile. "Another year rolls around soon, does it not?"

"Possibly. I hadn't thought about it," he lied, taking a fortifying sip of the smooth brandy. As if the day his father, the fourth baron, and his mother, a high-end courtesan turned baroness, perished in a terrible carriage accident wasn't permanently etched into his mind. "But enough chitchat, let's get this meeting underway so we can all get some sleep."

A soft knock sounded, and a livery-clad footman poked his head around the door. "Beg pardon, my lords, but there is a woman who wishes to speak to Sin."

Vice laughed. "Rather early for a morning call. Our Sin's legend is growing. I'll take wagers: three to one he's about to be sweet-talked into rescuing maid number thirty-two. Five to one he's pitchforked by that disgruntled abbess."

The footman vigorously shook his head. "Oh no, my lord. She ain't either of those. She's a countess. The Countess Carrington, her fancy little card said."

Every hair lifted from the back of Sin's neck. The title was familiar, but he couldn't picture the lady's face, and that was a warning in itself. "Tell me about her."

"Beautiful blonde. Young, the old earl's treat to himself. I know she's been stuck in the country for years, only came to town when he permitted it and only allowed out for select occasions. Her uncle is an acquaintance of yours, though: the Duke of Waverly."

"Ah," he said, frowning as the connections fell into place. What the hell was Grace Lloyd-Gates, bishop's daughter, dutiful wife, and excruciatingly virtuous widow doing at Fallen? Women like her usually refused to come within thirty feet of the building, unless of course they were waving placards. Perhaps she was here on a dare? Surely she couldn't be seeking membership.

Could she?

...

Unable to sit still for a minute, Grace circled the elegantly furnished parlor. On another occasion, another address, she might have curled up on the overstuffed chaise and gazed for hours at the exquisite paintings on the walls, or perhaps ran her fingers over the keys of the polished pianoforte.

Not today.

Today, her stomach was in knots, perspiration misted her skin, and only through some sort of miracle had her feet obeyed the command to walk up to Fallen's front door. It was one thing to ponder solutions, but being here at the entirely unfashionable hour of ten o'clock in the morning to begin the boldest, riskiest, most ill-thought out plan of her life, was something else entirely.

"Lady Carrington. My sincere apologies for keeping you waiting."

The rich, deep voice nearly made her jump a foot in the air, but straightening her shoulders, Grace turned in a swirl of lavender-striped skirts.

And nearly swooned.

It was him. The lord they called Sin was the same man she'd fantasized over since that long ago day in Hyde Park, and if anything, he was even more divine up close. Short-cropped chocolate brown hair, exotic amber eyes, strong, square jaw, perhaps a touch under six feet in height, but so broad in the shoulders he appeared much bigger. Under that shirt, trousers, and crisp cravat she would wager he was sculpted muscle all over.

"Good morning, Lord St. John," she replied quickly, trying to gather her scattered thoughts while ignoring her hardening nipples and an unfamiliar throbbing between her legs. "Thank you for seeing me at this hour and on such short notice. I know it is most, ah, irregular."

One eyebrow arched, but there was an unexpected kindness in his crooked grin. "I must admit, my lady, you are not someone I ever thought to welcome through Fallen's doors. Is there something I can assist you with?"

"Yes," she blurted, but the rest of her carefully rehearsed speech dried up, and she wanted to scream in frustration. This devastating man would hardly be inclined to assist a stranger behaving like a gormless twit.

"And that is?" he prompted.

Feeling a blush storm across her cheeks, Grace swallowed hard. "Forgive my hesitancy. It is a most delicate matter."

"Are you in trouble? Is your late husband's family causing you grief?"

"No. Nothing like that. It's my father. He...he has contracted me a second marriage to a most unsuitable man and I simply cannot do it."

The baron tilted his head, his expression curious. "Did you come here seeking an alternative husband, Countess? Because I have no desire whatsoever to marry, despite your obvious charms."

"No! Ah, no, my lord..." Grace broke off, and took a long, deep breath. *Courage, girl.* "What I would like, is for you to partially ruin me."

"*Partially* ruin you?" he said, amusement returning as he settled onto the nearby chaise, one booted foot resting casually across the other. "My dear lady, while you are absolutely in the right city and the right club for ruination, I'm not sure I understand the partially part."

"Oh dear, that did sound odd, didn't it? What I meant was, creating a mild scandal with, no offense intended, the most notorious rake in London, believable enough for my new fiancé to be so horrified he cries off and leaves me in peace."

"Countess—"

"Please, do call me Grace," she said, daring to take a few steps closer.

"Very well, Grace. You realize this plan has numerous glaring flaws? If this fellow is a man with any sort of sense, he wouldn't give you up for anything. Not even a, er, mild scandal with…come on, I'm only about fourth or fifth on London's notorious rake list…hmmm, perhaps third. But you're a widow, with a widow's experience and needs, not a silly chit fresh out of the schoolroom."

"The gentleman in question is Lord Baxter."

Lord St. John's lips tightened, and just for a moment something dark and dangerous swirled in his amber eyes. "*Baxter?*"

"You know him?"

"Indeed. A creature of the most stringent taste and morals, dedicated to cleansing society. That we could all be as purebred and without taint as him."

For the first time in days, true hope flared. "The wedding date is set for June first. I was permitted to come to town with just my maid-companion to have a new wardrobe measured. She is completely loyal and will make excuses for me if needed. And…and I can pay you! Here, take this, it is all I saved from my allowance," she said, striding forward to drop a drawstring purse into his lap.

"Grace," he said with a sigh, tossing the purse back to her. "Keep your pin money. If your mild scandal idea does work, we'll discuss terms once your situation is settled. Besides, I have a weakness for beautiful damsels in distress, and ladies forced into situations they have no desire to be in angers me. Especially when said situation involves men with...a highly inflated sense of entitlement."

She choked on a relieved sob. "Oh th-thank you. Thank you, thank y—"

"All right, pet, enough. Now, come and sit down and tell me exactly what you consider a mild scandal for partial ruination to include."

Lord St. John's tone was idle, yet those fascinating eyes were fixed on her with an unsettling directness, the kind of focus that implied he learned a person's strengths and weaknesses, truth and falsehood, in a heartbeat. If she answered with anything less than absolute honesty, he would know, and probably change his mind.

Grace sank onto the chaise next to him and stared at her clasped hands. "I'm not sure. But I know it must be public. Perhaps kissing and touching at a ball or in a carriage?"

His lips twitched. "Kissing and touching. I see."

"Is that so unexceptional here?" she said hotly, hating her own naïveté. "Do people walk around Mayfair wearing nothing but rouge and a smile nowadays? Are there lewd displays atop horseback on Rotten Row?"

"Restricted to Thursdays," St. John said, nodding gravely. "And not so popular a pastime in the winter months. Embarrassing for certain gentlemen, you understand."

"But never for you," she replied, then clapped her hand over her mouth. Where on earth had that comment come from?

He burst out laughing, a delightfully warm and hearty sound that spoke of humor regularly indulged. "Thank you, but saddle chafing and windburn are rather off-putting. I must admit to a definite preference for indoor fucking. Beds, desks, window seats, walls, chaises..."

Like this one? Grace's cheeks heated to boiling point. "I've only known the marriage bed. And that taught me relations between a man and woman meant enduring pain in darkness twice a week. But I'm *sure* there is so much more. There must be. My maid tells me women flock to you quite willing to risk all, so I imagine you offer a far different experience."

"Christ, Grace," he said, all humor vanishing as he took an audible breath. "Look at me."

"I can't."

"I said look at me."

Slowly, reluctantly, she lifted her head. His gaze was sympathetic, but barely leashed heat burned as well, making her gown feel far too tight. Seconds later, a rough, slightly callused fingertip dragged a tingling path of fire across her lower lip, then darted down to caress her collarbone and the lace-edged bodice of her gown.

Grace's nipples hardened further and she shivered. It should be embarrassing, how fast a brief, expert caress from a near-stranger aroused her, but all she could think of was offering anything he wanted to continue, mild scandal be damned. "My lord, please, I—"

"Lovers should be on a first name basis, even temporary, fake ones. Call me Sin."

"I am very grateful for your assistance."

He shrugged. "Well, it is a most intriguing challenge, devising a deliberate yet mild scandal for partial ruination. But in the interests of science and justice, I shall ponder some options. Regrettably I have a series of meetings today, but be here tomorrow morning at eleven, and do not be late. Tardiness results in penalties."

Grace nodded quickly, desire and relief and uncertainty coiling tightly within her.

The betrothal-ending mission had begun.

Chapter Two

Baxter. Goddamned fucking *Baxter*.

The hated name had pounded his mind all damned night, and not even a particularly bright and sunny morning could improve his temper.

Unclenching his fists, Sin let his gaze travel the length and breadth of his private parlor. He willed the soothing combination of pale blue silk walls, white velvet chaises, and gold trim to calm his senses. The thought of that monstrous sack of shit near any woman made him want to vomit, but for some reason the feeling in regard to Grace was doubled. Carrington hadn't quite smothered the spirit from his trophy spouse—some very intriguing glimpses of minx and unawakened desire had shone through yesterday—but Baxter would be the death of her.

As he'd been the death of Sara.

The fucking useless authorities had ruled it accidental, saying Baxter's poor, unlucky fiancé had been running to greet him, tumbled down some steps, and suffered a fatal head knock. As if steps left faded cane welts across backs and legs.

As if smitten young ladies delirious with happiness often sent tear-stained notes to their childhood playmate, begging for help to stop the wedding. He'd been hours too late to rescue Sara. But that would never happen again.

Breathe. In. Out. In. Out.

Flexing his fingers, Sin sat down at his treasured pianoforte. This particular instrument had belonged to his mother, and even now, he could hear her groan as he deliberately butchered one masterpiece after another in the hope she might excuse him to go fishing. It never worked. She would give him that reproving look, and say "Seb, my baby, the good Lord gave you a gift that cannot be wasted, so the sooner you master the tune, the sooner you can escape." Then he'd play the entire stack of music sheets without a single error and she would clasp her hands and sway in time, that sunshine smile on her face…

"What a beautiful piece. And you know it by heart, too."

His head shot up to see Grace standing awkwardly on the other side of the room, her reticule clutched tightly in her fingers. Fuck, she was beautiful. Not even the slate-gray gown of half-mourning she wore hid her curves, or dulled the golden curls piled atop her head and the sapphire blue of her eyes. If he had any say in the matter, Baxter would call Grace his wife when hell froze over.

"Good morning, sweetheart. Welcome to my parlor."

"Your butler let me in and escorted me here. I hope that is all right, I wasn't going to argue with someone the size of a cathedral and the look of an executioner."

Sin laughed, his fingers continuing to caress the keys of their own accord. "Diaz is a kitten until the moment of threat, at which point he turns into a starving tiger. Quite remarkable to watch. But unlike tigers, I promise not to bite if you come over here and join me."

She ambled forward. "What if I asked nicely?"

"Well, well, I was right. My lady does have some minx about her."

"You know next to nothing about me, *my lord*, except my uncle's title, my father's occupation, and the name of my late husband."

"Touché," he said mock-contritely, the pertness of her tone causing his cock to stir. "But you still aren't seated."

Grace eventually perched on the wide, cushioned bench beside him. "There. Happy now?"

Time to discover the true mettle of the lady. "Of course. Although my joy would be exponentially greater if you were spread naked across the lid. With a muse such as you, I'm sure I could do more than play music."

She gasped, but a spark of something remarkably like curiosity in her eyes said it was a habitual response rather than true outrage. "Do you think about nakedness all the time?" she said eventually, sternly.

"The governess tone from the lady who spoke of Mayfair nudity and saddle fucking yesterday? I'm disappointed. And in answer to the question, not all the time. When I am in meetings with bankers, lawyers, and Fallen's co-owners, or any time I speak to the Prince Regent, nakedness is about the last thing on my mind."

Grace bit her lip. Hard. "Well. Um…"

Hell, but her lower lip was plump and pink. Her nipples and clit would probably be the same color. Had she ever orgasmed? He got the feeling she wasn't a lady who indulged in self-pleasure, so possibly not. God. Would her first climax be with a sigh? A prolonged moan? A scream of delight?

Shaking his head to clear his mind before his erection became too blatant, Sin gave her a thoughtful look. "Why did you maul that beautiful lower lip rather than laugh? You wanted to."

"Oh, did I?"

He nudged her with his shoulder. "You know you did. And it's all right, I am amusing. People tell me all the time. Often in the guise of 'one more word and I'll cut out your tongue and feed it to the chickens,' but I know what they mean."

Grace quivered, a sound escaping before she pressed her knuckles to her mouth. "N-not funny."

"You're right. And we really do need a new topic of conversation before I start imagining a naked Prinny rooster flapping around Mayfair and squawking at the shortage of truly high class tongues."

She laughed. Not a delicate snort or ladylike titter, but a full-blooded laugh that made her eyes glow like night stars, and her ample breasts bob. He wanted her spread across a bed, a desk, a chaise, anything really, just so he could feast on her swollen nipples and wet cunt, bury his cock inside her, and hear that delight as ecstasy instead. For she would be a screamer, once that criminally repressed passion was unleashed, that couldn't be more goddamned obvious.

Fuck.

Not for you. Mild scandal. Baxter.

With those sobering thoughts in mind, he got up from the pianoforte so fast he nearly tipped the bench over.

"Sin? Is something wrong?"

"Not at all, pet," he replied, wanting to kick himself for the less than smooth maneuver. Even now he could see uncertainty replacing the laughter on her exquisite face as she withdrew back into herself. "Damned bench was starting to give me splinters, that's all. Why don't we retreat to the chaise over there and talk further about this mild scandal? Much more comfortable. I should know, since I've fallen asleep on the thing a few times."

"Very well," Grace said slowly, rising from the bench. She didn't touch him as she strolled by, not even with an inch of gown fabric, but the scent of rose soap, light and clean rather than a heavy, cloying cloud of perfume most ladies wore, teased his nose. All at once he wanted to unfasten her chignon and run his fingers through her blond curls to release more of the fragrance, lick every inch of her creamy skin to see how it tasted in different places.

What the fuck was wrong with him?

Sure, she was beautiful, but he knew hundreds of beautiful women, all infinitely more experienced and available.

He needed to pull himself together.

Fast.

...

She'd never felt so off-balance.

Forcing herself to move as though she was cool and calm, Grace made her way over to the chaise and sat down.

The more they had spoken on the pianoforte bench, the more comfortable she'd felt with Sin. When he started teasing her, her long-suppressed sense of the absurd positively twirled with glee. That the truly delicious man of countless daydreams was also able to make her laugh, well, she'd been about ready to climb onto his lap and beg him to let her stay. And for a moment he'd looked at her with such hunger, too, like he wanted to tear off her gown and do unspeakably good things to her body.

Then he'd backed away. No, not backed away, the third most infamous rake in London had practically flung himself across the room.

"So," said Sin, dropping onto the other end of the chaise and resting his arm along the back, ensuring several feet remained between them. "Let us speak of mild scandals."

Her gaze narrowed. "Am I truly that odious?"

"Excuse me?" he replied, shooting her an arrested glance.

"Any farther away and you'd be perched on the armrest. Although I imagine Lord Baxter would approve."

Sin tilted his head, eyes glinting. "A mild scandal, you told me. I am merely practicing."

"Ha!"

"Such a tone, Lady Carrington. One might begin to think you were reconsidering the mild part. Now. To the task at hand. How should you like it to play out?"

"A kiss," she said, irritable at her own transparency when she'd been able to mask herself so well in the past. "In public. Like in a phaeton, or while strolling in a park or perhaps in a box at the theater."

"All right. What kind of kiss?"

An incredulous laugh escaped. "You are asking *me* about kissing?"

He didn't smile. "Yes. There are many types, pet. Chaste kisses. Ones of friendship. Relief. A teasing kiss, nothing more than a vague promise. Then new desire, clumsy and hungry but still with the edge of non-consummation. And finally the raw carnality of lovers. What do you want Baxter to believe?"

Grace stared at Sin, mouth dry and heart pounding. Nell had been right. This was a man who knew every nuance of pleasure, utterly at ease with his knowledge and expertise. "I...I'm not sure."

"Well then. Why don't we try an experiment? Kiss me, and I'll tell you what it says."

For a long moment she hesitated. Sweet heaven she wanted to. Badly. But it had been so very long since she kissed someone she actually wanted to kiss; the secrets of finishing school seemed like a hundred years ago. What if she and Sin banged noses or foreheads? What if all she could demonstrate was friendship or lukewarm teasing? A mild scandal had seemed so easy. Perhaps it wasn't at all. "I'm woefully out of practice," she said awkwardly. "Probably not very seductive."

"I'll be the judge of that. Look, I'll even meet you halfway on the chaise. Shimmy closer, pet, and kiss me as though bloody Baxter was peering through the window right now."

Grace nodded, excitement coiling in her belly at the chance to have something she'd wanted for the longest time. Then she leaned across and carefully brushed her mouth against his, once, twice, before timidly touching the tip of her tongue to his lips. A low growl escaped him, and she jerked back. "I did it wrong, didn't I," she said tightly, embarrassed. What a countrified twit she must appear to someone of his experience. "I'm sorry."

"On the contrary. It was sweet and perfect. But sweet and perfect won't end an engagement. If we are to create a public scandal, you cannot hold back. You must give me your all, so any gossips looking on unequivocally believe that rather than the quiet, virtuous widow of repute, you are an independent, hot-blooded woman with reckless, *ungovernable* sexual needs. For that is the last kind of wife a man like Baxter wants."

"I understand. Can we try again?"

His smile was pure wickedness. "Oh, I *dare* you to."

Dizzy heat flooded her, and Grace licked her lips. As if the quiet challenge had woken her inner wanton from an endless sleep, slowly, deliberately, she moved on the chaise, hitching up her gown and straddling Sin's lap. His eyes flared in surprise then darkened with desire, and she shivered at the unfamiliar and utterly addictive sensation of power.

Cupping his face, Grace kissed his forehead, his cheeks, his stubbled jaw, tasting and exploring the salty warmth of his skin. Then she moved to his mouth, tracing and licking the hard lips so very different from her own, until he opened and sucked her tongue inside. Abruptly the kiss became something hot and wild, a light breeze to a violent storm. He wasn't gentle, nor did she want him to be, and she could only sigh with pleasure as one hand clamped around the back of her neck, the other on the small of her back, and he crushed her lips with his.

Oh God. This was the kiss she'd been dreaming of her whole life. Raw and brutal and wonderful. With a low whimper, she threaded her fingers through his silky, short-cropped hair, letting her knees slide farther apart so she sat closer to him, unable to stop herself from rubbing her hard, aching nipples against the rock-solid expanse of his chest.

"Sin," she gasped in frustration, when the light friction wasn't nearly enough.

"I know. I know what you need," he said hoarsely, and she moaned in gratitude when the hand at her back slid up over her hip to cup one breast, two fingers massaging her nipple through her bodice. But again, she soon wanted more.

"Harder," she demanded, the wanton refusing to be denied a second longer.

"So greedy, darling."

Yet there was nothing but approval in his voice, and when the two fingers delved under her bodice to pinch her nipple directly, it sent a jolt of fierce arousal straight to her dampening core and she arched, crying out. This was passion, what the ladies whispered about, what they craved and risked all for. And if he ever stopped, she would—

"Sinny!"

Horrified, Grace jerked around to stare at the amused-looking brunette who now lounged in the doorway to the parlor. Her glossy hair tumbled down her back and she wore just an emerald satin dressing gown that barely constrained Venus-like curves, but she remained utterly at ease. Who would dare just march in? Was the stunningly beautiful woman one of Sin's mistresses? Sweet heaven, she could actually see the brunette's nipples, big and dusky rose colored, but so soft-looking, like velvet.

Quickly, Grace turned away, her cheeks on fire.

"What is it, Charlotte?" said Sin, as he removed his hand from Grace's breast and straightened her bodice so expertly, she wanted to kick him. "And what the hell happened to knocking?"

"I did knock, several times, but you were obviously, well, distracted. Your harem is waiting for you."

His *harem*? Grace didn't realize she'd growled the word until Sin laughed and squeezed her hand.

"Don't give me that look, pet. I'm in charge of staff at Fallen, and my harem is the maids. Most days I'd say coven rather than harem, though."

"Aw, Sinny, don't pretend you don't love us to bits. I'll tell the girls you'll be there in *five minutes*, don't make me get out my crop, now," the brunette said firmly, blowing them a kiss, and strutting from the room.

"Crop?" Grace blurted. "Did she mean a riding crop? Does she use it on *people*?"

As soon as she said the words she wanted to take them back, it was hardly her business what happened here. But Sin didn't look annoyed. More…pleased.

"Charlotte is our resident dominatrix. That is a woman who takes the lead role in sexual play. And yes, she often uses a riding crop or other toys. Many men and women find it incredibly pleasurable to be whipped."

"They do? And what do you mean by toys? What kind?"

He grinned. "While I would adore to continue this glorious conversation and answer all your questions, I do actually have to get to the meeting."

"Oh. Of course. Sorry!" said Grace, awkwardly scrambling off his lap. How on earth did one leave a lover, anyway?

"I'm the one who should apologize. Completely forgot I changed the meeting day. But I'll suffer for my lapse," he said ruefully as his gaze dropped meaningfully downward.

"Oh dear." She bit back a wayward smile at the very large

bulge between his legs. She, Grace Carrington, had caused that.

"Besides, we can meet again tomorrow, correct? I think we've got more to discuss about mild scandals before we go public. And we'll need to practice our scenario."

Indeed.

She couldn't wait.

...

"Sin! Mary can't sing, she has a head cold and sounds like an addled rooster."

"Sin! Number 42 spurted all over my pirate queen costume, and now it's ruined."

"Sin! You tell Number 19 the next time he swings his cock in my face while I'm pourin' drinks, he's gonna find teeth marks and an inch missin'."

As he took his chair at the front of the spacious chamber they'd converted into a meeting room, Sin shook his head and regarded his harem of ex-prostitute maids with an exasperated yet fond smile. Although they drove him to drink some days, every complaint, all the banter, each belly laugh was a victory against the demons of their pasts. All had been assisted away from deplorable situations of cruel violence, rape, starvation, and poverty, where they were left on the streets to die if they became ill or pregnant.

At Fallen, every maid was paid well and chose her own destiny, whether it was a quiet life of sewing and fussing over guests, taking a lover, indulging in party games, or a combination of all three. Watching them heal, become confident and outspoken, and gain independence was a source of profound satisfaction.

Sure, vicious threats came in on a daily basis from pimps and bawds; on several occasions Sin had been lucky to escape the hellholes of London with just cuts and bruises after brawling with people who made a rabid wolf look placid. The so-called do-gooders were almost as bad, all refined taunts and threats, frantic placard-waving, and a propensity for hurling handy objects. But under no circumstances would he stop. Actually, perhaps he was acting in memory of his mother as Devil suggested—although her situation had been markedly different to the maids of the harem.

Sin held up a hand in a half-hearted attempt to halt the chatter. "One at a time, you ornery wenches. I've heard less fuss from a migrating gaggle of geese."

"Oooh, sounds like someone needs some warmed milk and a nap," called one maid from the back of the room.

"More like he needs his pipe drained," cackled another.

"Actually, it's both," said Charlotte, and he scowled at the gleeful look on her face, one that indicated she was about to update the harem in full graphic detail of what she had witnessed in the parlor. The domme dared a lot, thanks to her longstanding close friendship with Devil.

"All right, all right, let's get this meeting started," said Sin, hoping to distract her from her tale, and him from an erection that still refused to fully subside.

No such luck.

Charlotte beckoned the other maids closer. "Gather round, girls. Our Sinny has found himself a nice, young lady widow! Got her onto his lap and learning the true meaning of the word kiss, hell in a teacup, that much was clear. I knocked and knocked but they didn't hear me, and oh, you should have seen her sweet face when I barged in to remind him of the meeting. Scarlet like a virgin, bless her. Do you have details to add, my lord?"

He smiled blandly. "Not a single thing."

Immediately a chorus of pleas and arguments filled the room, along with chairs scraping and cambric gowns rustling as thirty-one determined maids settled into a semi-circle for a group interrogation. The whole bloody lot had been pestering him for years to find a 'bride of his station' and sire children for them to dote on. For some unknown reason, they couldn't grasp that a *ton* wife would never work; even with his title, no well-bred woman would tolerate a scandal-rich, liberal-minded cit for a husband, a man not only the son of a courtesan, but firmly dedicated to helping prostitutes and running Fallen.

Hell, they only needed to look at Devil's example. Their quiet, near-respectable mathematical genius tried marriage to a lovely society chit, and it had gone so catastrophically wrong that Eliza now lived hundreds of miles away. Besides, he was too much his father's son to want a wife and a mistress, so it was far easier to remain a bachelor and meet his varied sexual needs with a succession of uncomplicated wanton beauties.

He was jolted back to the present as the meeting room protests reached roof-lifting proportions.

"Come on, Sinny," demanded an older maid to his left. "Tell us. What is her name?"

"None of your bloody business." He reached for a sheet of paper on the nearby wide oak desk, and dipped a silver pen into an inkpot. "Now, what must be ordered from the modiste apart from a come-free pirate queen costume?"

All at once silence reigned, and he lifted his head to see thirty-one pairs of eyes regarding him with grave disappointment. Like he'd cancelled Christmas, stolen their sweets, *and* yelled at orphans.

"Enough with the sad pup looks," he said irritably, the current state of his cock and the thought of long, Grace-less hours until tomorrow morning shortening his temper. "There is no tale to tell."

"We just want you to be happy, my lord," said a young maid, with far too much knowledge in her eyes.

"I am happy," he barked. "I'll be even happier when a completed order can be delivered to Madame Alice. Besides, there really isn't anything to tell. I only just met Grace."

Fuck.

Throwing his pen aside, Sin let a fierce glare roam the meeting room. Thirty-one faces beamed back at him.

"Lady Carrington is a widow in a very complicated situation. I am assisting her, and in a fortnight's time the matter will be resolved and we'll part on amicable terms forever. That is all. Now, let's settle this order. Last name down will be running about after Prinny and his current favorites for the rest of the week."

A near stampede of women descended on his desk, and he almost smiled. Almost.

Except he couldn't stop thinking about Grace. Her mischievous wit and curiosity. The heady combination of rose-scented soap and aroused woman. Her gasps and moans and cries when he'd kissed and played with her.

Sin gritted his teeth and shifted uncomfortably in the high-backed chair. Steel rod had nothing on his cock at the moment. All the day needed now was Devil and Vice to stroll into the room, all arched eyebrows and mocking grins, to repeat their appalling quips about the joys of oiling rusty, shrieking Gates, and his brain might actually explode.

What the hell was everyone's problem, anyway?

It wasn't like entertaining a widow was a novelty. Fallen had long ago established a reputation as a sanctuary for any age and gender. Perhaps no women as innocent as Grace, or with her strict background, and maybe he rarely allowed others into his private parlor, but that was by the by. He could do whatever the fuck he liked. Always had. Always would. As he'd said to the maids, he was merely assisting a lady in need.

Nothing more.

Chapter Three

"Must say, Lady C, it will be a happy day when I don't have to dress you in plain gray or lavender anymore. Fine for the ladies who truly miss their husbands, but there isn't a soul in London who is sorry old Carrington passed. Especially not his heir."

Grace smiled grimly in the mirror at Nell. "I thought that, too, but yesterday afternoon's visit to the milliner...all that color and trim and those high-necked, long sleeved sketches made me feel quite ill. For if my plan fails, I am soon to be a wife again."

"Bah," spat Nell, as she styled Grace's hair into a neat chignon. "I still think you should ask Sin to drag the puffed up old boot to those haunted lands down Dartmoor way and leave him for the wildlife. It would be a sour, bony offering, but—"

"Better the wildlife nibble Lord Baxter than me?"

"Exactly. Then you could wed Sin and spend your days nibbling that fine figure of a man instead."

Even the thought made her entire body heat. She'd felt

Sin's trouser-covered erection between her legs, but what might it be like to hold his naked length in her hands? To taste and explore every inch of that big, hard body with her lips and tongue and make him come?

"No," she said very regretfully. "Our nibbling is strictly on a friendship basis. He made it very clear he is not the marrying kind."

"But not at all averse to kissing you senseless? Your lips must have wondered what on earth was going on."

Grace nodded ruefully. "Sadly true. I was dreadful to start, peck, peck like a little bird. But then…oh my. He still believes I would benefit from more practice, though, and we got interrupted discussing the plan, so that is why I'm going back today."

"Well, just mind that he doesn't spend inside you until I've found some of those sponges to soak in brandy. Now is not the time for a pregnancy."

"Nell!" she spluttered. "It is only kissing!"

Her maid snorted. "So that was the only thing that happened? He didn't touch you anywhere other than your face? Ha. Your ruby cheeks confess. And I think you should absolutely indulge should the opportunity arise…so to speak. No one need know."

Words of denial sprung to her lips and then faltered. "I thought about him all night. What I might do or say if it became more than kissing. And…I want to. I want this for myself, and have for the longest time."

"Of course you do," said Nell. "It's Sebastian bloody St. John. You know, if I were twenty years younger and had unlimited funds, I'd buy the pirate fantasy room at Fallen with a sign outside that said 'Dear Sin, enter and plunder at will.' Promise me you'll go in there one day, my lady. If I must live vicariously through you, I expect details to make my slippers melt."

Grace laughed. "A pirate fantasy room? Oh, come on, that is surely a Banbury Tale."

"My brother says it is true. Apparently he was at a soiree and overheard another group discussing it, he gave them quite the lecture on immorality. It drives the *ton* barmy how secret the membership list is kept, but every so often details about the club's activities escape, and it sends the city into a frenzy. Actually, if Prinny is a patron, it's no doubt him who leaks like a rusty bucket."

"No doubt," said Grace. Even in the wilds of Gloucester, they'd heard about the Prince's loose tongue. "We'd best be on our way. I know I've said it before, but I really do appreciate your discretion and willingness to, er, explore the city in my carriage for the next two weeks."

All humor left Nell's face. "I'm pleased to help. You know how I feel about your father and the feral bat he married. One elderly husband is quite enough for any woman, but attempting to saddle you with a second? Outrageous. I'm not sure I believe his claim that your uncle endorses this new arrangement, either. Perhaps you should pay an impromptu afternoon call on the duchess."

"Actually, as soon as we arrived in town I sent a note suggesting afternoon tea. I didn't specify the reason in case other eyes read it, and unfortunately, I haven't heard back yet. I hope Aunt Anne isn't cross with me. I always enjoyed her company, but Carrington rarely allowed me to come to town and it has been over a year since I saw her in person."

"You give the duchess too little credit. She is a very astute woman who probably understands more than you think. In the meantime, there is no point waiting here for the post."

A half hour later they descended on Portman Square. Waving Nell away, Grace hurried to Fallen's discreet back entrance and rapped the shiny brass knocker. Anticipation robbed her of the ability to stand still, and she found herself almost dancing a minuet on the steps waiting for admittance.

"Ah, Lady Carrington," said a soft, accented voice, and she nearly yelped in surprise at the mountain of a man now blocking the doorway. How could Fallen's butler, who was broader than Sin and surely must be six and a half feet tall, move so soundlessly?

"Oh, Diaz. Good heavens, you startled me," she said with an embarrassed laugh as she remembered Sin's kitten to starving tiger quip. The attractive Spaniard was polite and deferential, but his bald head, pierced ears, scarred cheek, and unblinking black stare did indeed speak of a deadliness only barely leashed.

"My apologies, *señora*. His lordship is waiting for you in his private parlor, if you'll follow me."

For the third day in a row, they moved along beautifully decorated hallways too fast to admire the gold-framed landscapes on the wall, or the thick Aubusson rugs devouring the heels of her slippers. Abruptly the butler stopped and knocked on the door to Sin's room, then opened it and gestured for her to go in.

Nodding her thanks, Grace took a deep breath and entered the parlor. Sin wasn't playing the pianoforte this time, but standing at a window that overlooked an enclosed garden. His fawn trousers and white linen shirt fitted his huge body to perfection, revealing to anyone who cared to comment that he had no need whatsoever for padding or corsets.

"Good morning," she said unsteadily, nerves and anticipation almost robbing her of voice.

He turned immediately, his brow furrowed. "You've changed your mind."

"No! No. But I wondered if…that is, if the mild scandal doesn't work, then I'll be married to Baxter until he dies. I have just under a fortnight now to call my own, and there are things I should like to know. Things I won't experience if I am married to that man. Do you think when we practice…it could be far more than mild?"

Sin was silent for the longest time. Then he tilted his head. "I'm disappointed, Grace."

Her heart plummeted at his cool, remote tone, the absence of any laughter on his face. "Wh-why? What is the matter?"

"It is five minutes past eleven. I told you, did I not, what would happen if you were late to our appointments?"

His words from their first meeting echoed in her ears.

Tardiness results in penalties.

Grace swallowed hard at her own foolishness. She'd thought he desired her, but obviously not. "You did. Are…are you going to send me home?"

Ignoring the question, Sin strolled forward, hands behind his back, coming to a halt two feet in front of her. "Have you been thinking of me, Grace? Is that why you want so much more than kisses?"

"Yes."

"In what way?"

She studied his handsome face, searching for a hint of kindness, any faint chance he might forgive her stupid lapse. But there was nothing, his entire expression could have been hewn from stone.

Dismay made her want to weep, and she bowed her head.

Only to see the bulge of his fully aroused manhood straining against his trousers.

Oh God. Sin was *teasing* her again! Upping the stakes in a deliciously bold game that promised rewards better than anything she'd dreamed of. Longing filled her, and before she could question the rightness or folly of her actions, she sank to her knees. "I've thought about how you pressed between my legs—"

"Me? You mean my cock? Say it."

"Yes," she whispered, clenching her thighs against a wave

of shameless lust. "Your cock was so big and hard under the fabric. I wondered what it might feel like naked in my hands. To kiss and stroke it until you came for me and I could taste your seed in my mouth."

Sin made a low growling sound, and one hand delved into her chignon. He roughly pulled the ribbon and pins free, then wound her loose blond curls around his fingers. "Grace…"

"Sin?" she said, gasping in stunned pleasure as he tugged on her hair, just hard enough to invoke a light prickle across her scalp. Sweet heaven. He hadn't even kissed her, and she was quivering.

A scorching amber gaze met hers. "Show me."

...

The sight of Grace on her knees, the desire and excitement in her eyes, was a true combination of heaven and hell. When eleven o'clock had come and gone he'd paced his parlor, wondering if something had happened to her, or if that bastard Baxter had shown up and played the fiancé card to steal her away. Then she'd arrived, all sweet smiles and lust-darkened eyes, and he'd been torn between bear hugging her and blistering her ears with a lecture to rival anything she experienced in finishing school. Damnation. How could someone he'd only known a few days call forth such a range of strong emotions?

And then she'd asked for a real affair.

His hand in her hair had been a method to regain control, to remind her who was in charge. Yet he wasn't. Not by any stretch of the imagination. In the next twenty seconds, begging her to free his painfully engorged cock from the constriction of his trousers and take him into her mouth, was as likely as the sun setting in the west.

Straightening his shoulders, Sin tugged again on her silky,

rose-scented hair. "I said show me. This is your chance for atonement, Grace."

Her hands lifted, clumsily unfastening his trousers in a way that dragged her knuckles back and forth against his erection. Christ. If he came from this most innocent form of sexual torture, he might as well retire from the pleasure business immediately.

"May…may I kiss your cock, Sin?"

A short nod was all he could manage, and finally, thankfully, she took him in her hands and leaned forward so her pink, plump lips brushed the swollen tip. Again and again she kissed him, moving her mouth so she hit a different spot each time. Now the side, then the base, an exquisite, prolonged trail of her lips along a prominent vein while she cupped his heavy balls.

"Stop," he said through gritted teeth, as he removed his hand from her hair and squeezed the base of his cock.

"Why? Am I doing it wrong? I'm sorry. I haven't much exp—"

"No. If you want a real affair, I want you undressed. Fully, so you can show me every inch of your beautiful body. How hard are your nipples, Grace? As hard as yesterday? Stand up so I can see."

"My clothing," she whispered, lifting her arms so he could remove her lavender-striped gown, turning so he could loosen her stays. "Is always too tight when I'm here."

He smiled. "Then by all means, take off your chemise."

In one inelegant movement the garment lay on the floor. Instinctively, one arm crossed her breasts and another covered her pussy, then she took an audible breath, lifted her chin, and dropped her arms to her sides.

Hell.

She was even more perfect than he imagined. Full breasts with large, pale pink nipples. Narrow waist, flaring hips, and a thatch of visibly damp blond curls between her shapely legs. His cock surged and pulsed at the thought of being buried deep in that sweet, tight heat, and a drop of pre-come appeared on the head. Catching it with his thumb, Sin was about to flick the moisture away, when Grace touched his wrist.

"Please."

Wordlessly, he offered it to her, and she licked her lips before darting out her pointed little tongue and lapping his thumb clean.

Fuck.

Taking her hand, he near-dragged her over to a chaise, sitting her down so her mouth was at the exact same height as his cock.

"Suck me," he ordered in a voice so hoarse and strained it was a wonder she could even understand him. But she did, and soon she held his cock in her hand while she wrapped her lips around the swollen tip. Unable to stop himself, his fingers again tangled in her hair, guiding her head while his cock glided an inch farther into her avid mouth.

Grace made a humming sound of pleasure and he groaned at the added sensation, murmuring words of praise, of instruction, to use her tongue on the underside, to hollow her cheeks for stronger suction. Now utterly incapable of restraint, he began fucking her mouth with rough, unsteady strokes, and she was taking it, oh Christ, she was reveling in it. Inexpertly but greedily sucking him deeper while one hand cupped and stroked his balls.

"Yes, sweetheart. You're sucking me so good. I'm going to...fuck," Sin snarled, a guttural cry torn from his very depths as every muscle tightened then released in waves of pure ecstasy, and his come gushed down her throat in several long, violent streams.

Panting, his legs about to fold beneath him, he reluctantly withdrew his cock from Grace's eager mouth and collapsed on the chaise beside her.

It made no sense whatsoever that the most inexperienced woman he'd ever been with had given him the most intense orgasm, but here she sat, this bishop's daughter, this picture-perfect widow from the back end of bloody Gloucester. Already he could feel himself hardening again at the thought of having her under him, over him, hell, any way she wanted.

"Sin," she purred, her eyes sparkling as she ran her fingernails along his abdomen and stroked his trail of dark hair, "could you—"

"No," he replied, trapping her hands in one of his, a gentle grip, but one she wouldn't be able to free herself from.

"*No?*"

Sin's lips twitched as acute dismay replaced the fevered lust on her face. He'd never met a *ton* woman so refreshingly lacking in guile, and knowing all her responses were genuine only added to her charm. "That's right, no. If I let you come, it is not much of a penalty for your lateness, is it?"

"It was only five minutes!"

He *tsked*, using his free hand to rub the lightest of circles along her upper thigh. "Wouldn't matter if it was one minute, angel. When I give you an instruction, I expect it to be followed."

Grace slumped back on the chaise, the velvet cushions arching her so those lush, creamy breasts thrust forward. Tempted beyond measure, he lifted his hand and traced both taut pink nipples, circling and chafing the tender flesh with thumb and forefinger.

"Oh," she whimpered, beginning to writhe when he alternately stroked and pinched the hard peaks until they darkened to decadent raspberry. To continue the torment, he pushed her wrists above her head, arching her back farther so her right nipple was close enough to suck.

But he didn't, merely flicked his tongue over it and

scraped it with his teeth. His free hand dropped back down to caress her inner thighs, up and down and around, brushing her golden pussy hair but never touching her soaked, swollen labia and clit.

Grace cried out, her hips thrusting upward in an attempt to grind against his fingers, her rock hard nipple nudging his lips, two wordless pleas for mercy.

"You want me to suck those pretty pink nipples, sweetheart? A rough, fast finger-fuck? Or perhaps you just need my tongue buried very, very deep in your sweet, wet cunt. If that is the case," he finished, slowly licking his lips, "then beg me."

...

She'd never known desire could be so painful. So all-consuming.

Aroused to the point of madness, her skin coated in light perspiration and pearly moisture actually trickling from her center onto her inner thighs, nothing else mattered. Lord Baxter, an impending marriage, her father and stepmother's betrayal, all faded to the background against the driving need to come at once. One stroke of her throbbing clit could hurl her from the knife-edge into a brutal and prolonged climax, but Sin continued to deny her that relief, or even the ability to rebel against the teachings of a lifetime and touch herself.

"I'll do anything. *Please*," Grace murmured, so enslaved to the demands of her own body that tears gathered in her eyes.

"Please what, sweetheart?" he said idly, grazing light kisses against her cheeks and chin.

Her tongue flicked out to taste his jaw, and brushed Sin's mouth. He swore and suddenly her lips were taken by his in the harshest, most erotic kiss of her life. His hard lips demanded, his tongue plundered, and she struggled against the firm grip on her wrists, desperate to hold him, to run her fingers through his hair, to rip his shirt away so she could rub her aching breasts against his hot, hair-dusted chest.

Tearing her mouth away from his, she gasped, "Sin, oh God, please…"

He smiled, stroking her cheek, then her collarbone with a fingertip. "You have such beautiful breasts, Grace. So full and soft, and those nipples…look how engorged they are now, and how dark. Almost wine colored. I'm going to suck them. Suck and bite and lick them until they are so tender even the slightest touch makes you scream."

It took nary a minute and her broken cries were echoing through the parlor. His relentless mouth on her nipples was an exquisitely pleasurable torment, every teasing lap, every masterful scrape and tug a pulsing ecstasy between her legs.

But she needed so much more.

"Put your tongue in me," Grace pleaded, almost mindless with want. Later she could be shocked at asking for something so intimate, but not right now. "Down there, like you said."

"Down there? Oh, angel, I have no idea what you are talking about. But if you happened to specify pussy or cunt, or say, asked me to suck the swollen little nub of your clit, there'd be no confusion and I'd be happy to oblige."

Even though she'd never spoken those words in her life, her core thrummed in response. She moaned, her world reduced to one excruciating craving that would send her tumbling toward something cataclysmic. Proper behavior, society, mild scandals…they could all be damned. "Please," she begged. "Put your tongue in my pussy. Suck my clit. Make me come, darling, please."

Sin stilled, and a kind of panic engulfed her that he might stop, that he might inflict the ultimate punishment for her tardiness and abandon her on the verge of climax. But then he released her hands and slid down until he knelt in front of the chaise. Roughly, he gripped her waist and pulled her to the edge, forcing her thighs wide with his massive shoulders so one leg rested on the padded velvet arm of the chaise, the other dangled down his back. The position left her utterly open and defenseless, yet somehow she didn't feel vulnerable or ashamed. Just wildly excited.

Using his thumbs, he gently parted her slick, petal-soft folds, and Grace shuddered, arching her hips in wordless entreaty.

Leaning forward, Sin blew softly on her throbbing, aching flesh, then holding her gaze, he licked her pussy in one slow lap.

She screamed.

He licked her again and again, long, decadent curls of his tongue that reached as far up as her clit, and returned to plunge deeply into her pussy, making her moan and pant as relief and blissful pressure twisted together and hurtled toward breaking point.

"Yes, sweetheart," growled Sin between licks, "that's right. I want to hear how it feels when my tongue is buried in your cunt. Fuck, you're so wet and hot and taste so damned good…"

"Sin," said Grace hoarsely, her fingers threading through his hair and gripping his head as she writhed against his mouth. "I'm so close, oh please, oh God, let me come…"

He rammed his tongue inside her, pinched her engorged clit, and suddenly she was there. Waves and waves of unending pleasure that made her whole body jerk, and tore a prolonged cry of complete abandonment from her throat. Minutes later, or perhaps hours, it was hard to know, Grace stared at Sin with heavy-lidded eyes that could barely focus. He remained between her thighs, the knuckles of his index and middle finger rubbing soft, slow, achingly good circles between her pussy entrance and clit.

"Welcome back," he said with a grin. "Don't suppose you'd let me up now, these polished wood floors are hell on the knees after a while."

Fiery heat burned along her cheeks as she realized her leg was still draped over his shoulder, with her heel practically having gouged a moat in his back. Not to mention her hands' unwillingness to surrender their grip on either side of his head.

Oh sweet heaven.

"I'm terribly sorry," she mumbled, freeing him and stumbling across the parlor to slip on her chemise so she wasn't so blasted *naked*.

"No need for apologies. In fact, based on our undeniable chemistry, I am quite convinced the time has come to go public and create that scandal…but perhaps not so mild? What do you think?"

Grace stared at him, torn. June first was only ten days away, so the sooner they damaged her reputation, the better. But oh, the temptation to ignore the harsh reality of arranged marriages and filial duty, and instead stay cocooned and happy within the sanctuary that was Fallen. "Are you sure I'm ready?"

"Absolutely. Any more ready and we both might combust. I was mulling over the best time and location, and believe tomorrow night at Vauxhall Gardens would suit our purposes admirably. We could have supper, listen to the orchestras, watch the fireworks…and create some of our own," he finished with a wicked grin.

"There will no doubt be a lot of people."

He nodded. "Thousands. From all levels of society. If we are shockingly indiscreet in front of some *ton* stalwarts then plead with them to keep our affair secret, the news will cross London in an hour at most."

"That slow?" said Grace with a reluctant laugh. "I'm disappointed."

Sin's amber gaze kindled, almost a caress in itself. "Perhaps I could offer a sweetener then. Would you care for a tour of Fallen before we venture out together?"

Oh.

"I would like that very much," she replied, aiming for a casual tone rather than intensely curious and debutante-giddy. "Although my maid Nell is going to be heartbroken when I tell her the pirate fantasy room is just a rumor made up by feeble-brained gossips."

A slow smile spread across his face. "Indeed. Just a rumor."

Grace's jaw dropped. "Wait a minute. Are you saying—"

"I'm saying you need to return tomorrow night, eight o'clock sharp. Diaz will fetch you a numbered mask to wear before you leave. And sweetheart…"

"Yes?"

"Do *not* be late. Next time I won't be so…forgiving."

She nodded. "As you wish."

Chapter Four

Tossing the latest batch of threatening notes into the flames dancing in his parlor fireplace, Sin watched them burn with a grim smile. A saner, more intelligent man might have taken the hint and stopped his activities long ago, but adding to the harem was too satisfying. Just a few weeks ago, he'd reunited sisters after three years forced separation. The copious tears, the incredulous joy as elder cradled younger and crooned guarantees of warmth and food and safety, ensured no bawd, pimp, or rabid clergyman would stop him. Not while he had guineas to spend, and God knew he had mountains of those.

"Sin?" said Devil, poking his head around the door. "Hurry up, Vice is asking for your opinion on two members. Seems an heir and spare both have a problem with Scots and maids who say no."

He scowled at Devil from across the room. "Who is the heir?"

"Dunbar."

"Cancel both memberships immediately, and their father's, too, no refund. Vice's word is law on the floor, no questions asked. And for God's sake, Dev, take a bath and shave. You have ink on your nose. Also, comb your damned hair and buy some new cravats, you look like you crawled out from under a bridge."

"I do?" said Devil, blinking as he pushed gold-rimmed spectacles higher up his nose with one finger. "Damnation. Eliza always used to remind—"

Sin sighed as his friend's words abruptly halted. "When are you going to stop being such a bloody numbskull and fetch your wife from the country? It's painfully obvious you adore her, even if she is human rather than guinea or promissory note."

"On the contrary," said Devil, his face and tone now frigid. "I do not. She was a mistake I cannot rectify, and her last letter indicates contentment, so mind your own business. Oh, and by the by, your countess has just arrived."

"She's not my countess," he replied, forcing himself to stroll rather than sprint toward the door.

Devil snorted. "The harem swears differently."

"Christ Almighty. Is there no loyalty in the world anymore?"

"Well, I do pay their wages and expenses. Plus, they inform me I am so kind and adorable that the hordes who claim I'm as black-hearted as my namesake must never have met me. I think it is the spectacles and ink spots."

"My stomach is officially churned. Go settle the accounts before I cast up mine."

With Dev's mocking laughter following him down the hallway, Sin made his way downstairs to the side entrance foyer. A glance at the stately grandfather clock in the corner indicated it was a quarter to eight, and a smile tugged at his lips.

Grace was early.

Although Fallen opened to members at seven o'clock in

the evening each Monday, Wednesday, and Friday, it didn't usually get frantically busy until after ten. Now was the perfect time for a tour, to perhaps see a performance or introduce her to the many different pleasure and fantasy rooms.

"Hello, Sin."

She stood alone in a simple lavender evening gown, her blond curls fastened atop her head with an amethyst clip, small white teeth worrying her lower lip. Thankfully, her black and white satin demi mask sat securely in place as she took in the opulent surroundings, the exquisitely dressed and bejeweled members of the *ton* laughing and chatting as Diaz checked their tickets and masks at the door.

"Welcome," he said briskly, taking her gloved hands in his. "Don't be nervous, although you'll probably see some shocking things, for the men and women who pay to entertain themselves here have a wide variety of tastes and needs. But let me reassure you that all acts are consensual. No one, staff or guest, is under any compulsion to take part in or watch something they do not wish to."

Grace trembled, and he used a finger to lift her chin so her sapphire gaze met his. But there was no fear or revulsion there, just banked heat.

"Sin," she said quietly.

"Yes, sweetheart?"

"I couldn't sleep last night. I couldn't concentrate on anything today, even when Lord Baxter made an unexpected tea and lecture visit and stayed two blasted hours. Now I know what it feels like to come, I want…I want *more*."

When her voice trailed off, he leaned close and nipped the side of her throat, making her gasp.

"Tell me what more means for you," he murmured. "This won't go any further, and it's not like I'm in any position to judge, so you may as well unburden yourself."

"It's shocking. I mean…not usual."

"Must I invoke penalties for coyness as well as tardiness?"

A dark blush spread across her delicate cheekbones. "Very well. I want to watch. Other ladies, I mean. I want to watch them come, see what they look like, how they sound compared to me."

"Indeed?"

She nodded, then buried her face in his shoulder. "I've never told anyone this, but years ago at my finishing academy, there was another student. A very pretty redhead."

Christ, yes. "Do continue, my dear. With no detail spared."

"Well…in secret, we used to practice kissing. For when we made our debuts and waded through countless male admirers, you see. Any spare hour we'd steal away, hold hands, and practice until our lips and tongues hurt."

"Go on. That is a mild confession."

"Ha! One evening she loosened my nightgown and kissed my breasts the way she kissed my mouth. I was shocked, but my nipples were so tender, and the way she licked and rubbed them with her tongue felt so good…I didn't even think about stopping her."

Resisting the urge to adjust his hardening cock, Sin instead curved his hand around her waist, pulling Grace even closer. "Let me guess. All went well until your body demanded more."

"Yes," she whispered, shivering. "When I got hot all over, and that throbbing and dampness started between my legs, I didn't know why. I was confused and a bit frightened, and the guilt set in that another girl was touching me so intimately. So I pushed her away and ran, avoiding her completely until term break. Not long after, her family moved to Switzerland, so I couldn't apologize or explore further."

"And I take it you've always regretted missing out on experiencing a girl sucking your nipples or fingering your pussy and making you come? And to do the same for her?"

Grace sighed. "Sometimes I dream about it. What it might be like. And I want to know, I really do."

He stifled a guttural groan. Like a true masochist, he had to fucking ask, and this sweet, beautiful woman painted a picture of sensuality so erotic his engorged cock was about to split open his trousers. Well. This inequality simply wouldn't do.

"Come with me," Sin said abruptly. "We'll get to your redhead, but you clearly need more than what we've done so far."

"Are we starting the tour?"

"In a manner of speaking," he replied, tucking Grace's arm through his and leading her across the marble floor and through the solid oak door leading to the private rooms. They walked along a long, narrow hallway, past several doors, until they reached a bolted one. Sin retrieved a brass key from his waistcoat pocket and unlocked it, then tugged her inside the large, candlelit space.

Grace sucked in a sharp breath. "My goodness."

He inclined his head, finally regaining some control. "You asked me about toys the other day, this is what I meant. Everything is stored in this chamber: whips, crops, dildos, beads, balls, blindfolds, silken cord for restraints, feathers, costumes, masks, oils and lotions, crosses…all purchased weekly for our discerning guests."

"Are all these things used together?"

"No," said Sin, with a bark of laughter. "Although perhaps I might set that as a future challenge, everything in one night secures a life membership. With an audience to ensure the result is all above board, of course."

She blushed. "Do…do you have a favorite toy?"

Sin tilted his head. "An excellent question, sweetheart. But I'd rather you look around and point out what interests you."

Her eyes widened, but the rampant curiosity that heated his blood reappeared, and she stepped past him to peruse the room. The wooden crosses and leather whips she passed without a second glance, instead pausing at the velvet-lined trays of gold-tipped, carved jade dildos. "Why are they all different sizes?"

"Different sizes for different needs."

"Really? Surely no one would choose the small ones."

Strolling over, Sin halted behind Grace, pleased when she leaned back against him. "Those aren't for your pussy, sweetheart, but your ass."

"*What?*"

"Our lady guests tell me that when they have a dildo inserted there, sensation everywhere else is heightened and their orgasm is twice as powerful and prolonged."

Grace visibly swallowed at his words, turning in his arms to give him that violently arousing look of blended desire and pleading. "Show me?"

He smiled. "Your wish is my command."

. . .

Just when she thought she couldn't be any wilder or more wicked, Sin would introduce her to a new wonder. And if this evening successfully damaged her reputation and ended their affair, then by heaven she would indulge in everything possible beforehand. Create enough beautiful sexual memories to last a lifetime.

Her breathing ragged with excitement, Grace watched him select one of the jade dildos and a clear glass bottle of pale golden oil. "Are we going to retire to a chamber?"

"No time, pet. But I'd like to suggest a little game of anticipation. Should you win, you will have countless orgasms."

She wrinkled her nose suspiciously. That sounded entirely

too easy. "And what does the game involve?"

"Wearing this dildo inside you when we go out. No one will know but us, of course."

Sin's tone was so casual, and his half smile indicated he fully expected her to decline. Well. Tonight there was a reckless moon rising, and Grace Lloyd-Gates Carrington would dance under it.

"All right," she said calmly. "You'll need to put it in for me, though. Should I bend over? Or kneel on something?"

His eyes widened, then closed briefly. "The table," he said in a voice so hoarse, she smiled inwardly. "On your hands and knees."

Nodding, Grace hitched up her gown and scrambled onto the narrow wooden structure. There were a few ruby red satin cushions, and she tucked one under her knees, and the other under her elbows. Sin carefully scooped up her gown and rolled it so it fell in folds across her back, but left her bottom exposed to the cool air.

There was a long pause, and she glanced over her shoulder uncertainly as embarrassment began to defeat confidence. "Well?"

"Give me a moment. I'm admiring perfection and testing my own willpower."

Relieved, Grace wiggled her bottom mischievously and shifted on the cushion so her thighs were spread a little wider. Sweet heaven, he made her feel like the most beautiful and seductive woman in England. "Is that better?"

Sin cursed, his breathing irregular, before one blunt finger began stroking her pussy, pushing past her labia and circling in the wetness there. But he didn't venture inside her, even when she arched to give him greater access, just teased and rubbed until slickness decorated her inner thighs.

"I'm going to start with my fingertip in your ass," he said in a rough voice that somehow soothed and aroused. "It's soaked in your juices so should be easy. When you're ready, I'll insert the dildo."

"I trust you," Grace said huskily, arching her back in welcome. "Do it."

His finger delved again, this time trailing back and rubbing the moisture against the tight untouched opening, and she squirmed. How could *that* be such a pleasurable spot?

"All right?" Sin murmured, as he pushed his fingertip inside her.

"Ahhh," she said, jerking.

He stopped. "Does it hurt?"

"No. I don't know. It just feels so…so different. But keep going. Please."

Slowly, carefully, he scooped more moisture and rubbed and pressed, inching his finger a little more into her backside each time. It burned a little as he stretched her, yet the heated friction and sheer fullness when he thrust back and forth was so good it made her whimper, and soon her hips were grinding against him to intensify the sensation.

"More, Grace?"

"Mmmm," she begged. "Yes. The dildo. Put it in me."

Another pause, the pop of a bottle uncorked, and a light stream of cool, citrus-scented liquid trickled onto her warm flesh. More pleasured whimpers escaped as Sin expertly prepared her back entrance with the oil, but the sound became a guttural groan when he began pushing the jade dildo inside her.

Oh God.

It was thicker than Sin's finger, and shockingly different. Smooth and unforgiving, and lacking the skin on skin connection to Sin that she'd come to crave, the cold, cylindrical object forced her delicate inner walls to melt around it, tormenting her already stimulated flesh to breaking point.

Writhing, desperate, Grace balanced on one elbow and

lifted an unsteady hand to slide between her legs. Just one touch. One pinch of her clit and she would come so hard the Vauxhall Gardens fireworks would pale in comparison.

Without warning, her world twisted and turned, and she shrieked in frustration at being swept off the table and set on her feet.

"Sweetheart," Sin chided, his eyes gleaming. "Surely you must know that touching yourself is cheating. Now, walk for me."

Shooting him a murderous look, Grace took her usual stride. And stumbled against him with a low cry, as the dildo shifted and sent a fierce jolt of agonizing pleasure through her body.

"It's too much," she panted, when the throbbing eased to bearable. "I can't."

"Incorrect. A lady of your mettle can achieve anything," he replied, the brusque certainty in his tone curling around her heart, making her even wetter. "Around this room, then back down the hallway, and off we'll trot to Vauxhall."

"Very well," she said through gritted teeth, trying much smaller steps this time. Definitely better, although the pressure and fullness of the jade remained an inescapable, dizzying presence inside her.

When Sin offered his arm she took it, and they walked slowly back through the foyer and outside to his waiting town carriage. The act of climbing two wobbling fold-down steps, and perching awkwardly on the luxurious cream leather squabs nearly broke her, but when the carriage lurched into a familiar swaying, rocking motion as it travelled down the uneven cobbled street, Grace gripped Sin's hand with a brittle sob.

Seconds later she lay back against the cushioned seat, one now slipperless foot balanced on the butter-soft leather, the other on the ground, her skirts around her waist and Sin kneeling between her spread thighs.

"I'm sorry," he said gruffly. "I'm a fucking idiot. It is too much with the carriage. Here, I'll take the dildo out and—"

"No."

Sin froze. "No? But you aren't enjoying it."

Panting against the constant rocking stimulation, Grace managed to lift a hand and cup his cheek. "What I'm not enjoying is being empty when I could be crammed full with your cock. A toy isn't nearly enough, not when you could be touching me…inside me. I need you. And I think you need me, too, judging by the bulge about to tear your trousers to pieces."

"I've been hard as fucking stone since you first walked into Fallen," he bit out, his shoulders rigid with tension, his eyes glittering. "Do you even know how erotic the contrast was, that drab, loose mourning gown with your wicked laugh and minx tongue? I think of you even when I shouldn't. Your scent…the way you taste…fucking haunts me."

Joy enveloped her, making her bold. "Well then," she said softly, dropping her hand to stroke the soft, damp skin of her inner thighs, further encouraged by his ragged indrawn breath. "What *are* we going to do, when I'm so wet and you're so very hard?"

Sin unfastened his trousers and took his erection in hand, pumping it once, then again. His cock looked even thicker and longer than yesterday, the veins prominent and pearly moisture dripping from the swollen tip.

"I just don't know," he said wickedly, trailing the head over her labia and clit, combining their juices until she moaned, surely loud enough for the driver to hear. Her core throbbed, the dildo seemed to throb, too, and she shuddered at the clawing hunger to feel him buried inside her at once.

This was real. What she had been missing her whole life, and whatever happened with Lord Baxter, this would remain with her for always.

"Please," she whispered. "I want it so badly. To be joined

with you…a new memory to wash away those other years. Please, Sebastian. Don't make me wait anymore."

Molten amber eyes met hers, and she cried out as he fitted the head of his cock to her pussy entrance and thrust deep and hard. The brutal movement ground against the dildo in her backside, stretching and filling her to an intoxicating point just below pain, the burn of the double penetration somehow heightening the shocking pleasure.

"Come for me, darling. I want to feel your tight cunt milk my cock," he growled, and she climaxed with a low scream, a violent, full body orgasm that broke her apart and yet mended her at the same time.

But he didn't pause, just continued the deliciously rough lunge and withdrawal in tandem with the rocking of the carriage, grinding the base of his cock against her tender clit and sending her tumbling into ecstasy again and again. Only after her third orgasm did Sin pull out of her body and come himself, long, warm spurts of creamy seed that thoroughly coated her mound and lower belly.

"Fuck, Gracie," he gasped, falling back against the corner of the carriage. If Grace had possessed the energy, she might have grinned at the stunned surprise in his eyes, the utter satiation. Not to mention her own glow at the nickname. No one had ever called her Gracie, and from his lips it turned her old fashioned name into something playful. Sensual. *Special*.

"Shall I…um…" she ventured as the silence lengthened, only broken by uneven breaths and fabric rustling as Sin leisurely righted his clothing.

"No. I'm savoring the view. If I were an artist I would paint you just so…sapphire eyes shining, pink and perspiring cheeks, legs spread wide to show your swollen, pleasured cunt and the dildo embedded in your ass, my come marking your skin. Christ. I'd call it '*Wicked Angel or The Only Way to Travel*.'"

Grace blushed, feeling more beautiful in her disheveled

state than she ever had in watered silk and jewelry. "I'm not sure they'll let me into the Gardens in my current state, though."

"Good point. And if another man saw you like this, I would have to…"

"Yes?" she said softly when his words trailed off, hope twining around her thudding heart. *Say it. Say you don't want our affair to end, even if this plan works.* "You would have to what?"

"Never mind," Sin replied, frowning. "Now, let's get you tidied up."

Head bowed because she couldn't mask her acute disappointment, Grace sat still as he procured a large linen handkerchief and wiped all traces of his seed from her body, then withdrew the jade dildo from her backside and dropped it into a small storage pouch cleverly hidden between the squabs and side of the carriage. No sooner had Sin discarded the handkerchief, the carriage came to a shuddering halt.

A glance out the window confirmed they had indeed arrived at Vauxhall Gardens, and nerves and sadness twinged in her belly.

This was it then. The beginning of the end.

...

Even though he'd been here countless times, Vauxhall Gardens remained one of Sin's favorite places in London. It was loud, frenetic, and colorful, as only an open air venue that served thousands of people could be. But the haphazard blend of traditional activities like music and dancing, and fascinatingly modern like gas balloon flights, plus the Palladian, Gothic, and exotic architecture, always soothed his senses for some unknown reason.

Sin handed two crowns to the lad at the gate to cover the

entry fee of three shillings and sixpence each, then tucking Grace's arm securely through his, continued down the Grand Walk. God knew his senses needed soothing after the heady visit to the toy room and the subsequent carriage ride. Merely the most intense, powerful, exquisite fuck of his life. The way Grace's wet cunt gripped him while the jade dildo stimulated the underside of his cock through the thinnest of walls…Hell, it was no wonder he'd ejaculated what felt like a half gallon of come onto her stomach.

What he hadn't expected was the utter recoil against another man witnessing her post-orgasmic state, or being the reason she lay so flushed and panting and boneless. Which was ridiculous. As soon as they shoved Baxter off the prospective marital cart, Grace would leave and meet someone new. A no doubt bloody perfect, respectable, conservative man of impeccable lineage approved by her family and whom she would love, a man who would marry her, share her bed, fill her over and over until her belly swelled with child…

Fuck.

"Oh my word," Grace breathed, and he looked down with a scowl at the astonishment in her eyes.

"What? You've been here before, surely," he replied in a too-clipped tone, even more irritated at the idiotic direction his thoughts had taken.

She shook her head. "No, not ever. Carrington thought it far too vulgar. Especially the fact that it is open to everyone, not just the wellborn. And before that, on the odd occasions my father and stepmother brought me to London, it was only to visit relatives."

"Your late husband was a carbuncle on the ass of the world. Much like Baxter. Well then, allow me to be your tour guide for the evening. What would you like to see first? The art gallery has some fine works by Hogarth and Hayman. Or we could stroll by the orchestra and listen to music. Although it might pay to have supper first before everything is devoured. This is your chance to enjoy ham sliced so thin you could read a book through it."

Grace smiled. "Supper it is. I must admit, I'd dearly love some sweets—"

"Sin. Sin, dear boy! Over here!"

At the familiar raucous and rather slurred hail, he glanced over to the supper boxes and raised a hand in greeting to their future king. But before he could say a word, Grace tugged hard on his arm.

"That is the *Prince of Wales*," she whispered, her eyes like saucers. "You really know him?"

"I do. Come and meet him."

"What? No! We can't just march into the royal box."

"On the contrary, darling. Prinny will think it unpardonably rude if we don't. Besides, we need the loosest tongue in England on our side tonight, correct?"

To his surprise, Grace hesitated. "Well…"

His gut clenched hard. "Are you having second thoughts about the plan? About Baxter?"

"I, ah," she whispered, looking away. Then she straightened her shoulders and re-met his gaze. "No. I just panicked at the thought of meeting royalty. I'm sorry, Sin."

"You called me Sebastian in the carriage."

"I did?"

"Yes," he replied, leaning close, unable to stop himself tucking a loose curl behind her ear and stroking her cheek. "When you begged me to fill your pussy because you were so wet and aching you couldn't bear it anymore. I liked it."

Grace shivered. "I like your real name. It's gallant. Sensual. But solid, too."

Sucking in a deep breath, Sin glanced back to where Prinny was now impatiently beckoning them to approach. If he stared any longer at the lavender silk barely constraining Grace's visibly hard nipples, he might shove her up against a pillar, tear her gown, and feast on them before fucking her senseless again. Christ. What the bloody hell was wrong with him? He was behaving like a rash young buck on his first night out.

"Come on. If we don't hurry, we'll be in the Prince's disfavor, and believe me, that is not a place you want to exist. He's a charming friend, but his grudges hold fast for a very long time, even the petty ones."

Guiding her across to the royal box, Sin bowed low, feeling rather than seeing Grace execute a perfect curtsy beside him.

"You took your time, Sin. Thought you were giving me the cut direct for a while there. Most shabby," said the Prince of Wales in an ominously petulant tone, when Sin was standing straight again.

"My fault, your royal highness," said Grace, blinking up at the prince, her eyes sapphire pools and her smile sweeter than honey. "I was altogether overcome at the thought of meeting you."

"Looked more like you were overcome at what Sin was doing. Don't think you would have minded at all if he'd thrown you over his shoulder and rushed off to one of those darkened walkways, what? Ha! Are you new to the harem?"

Color streaked across Grace's cheeks. "I am…not an employee, your royal highness."

Prinny's eyes bulged. "Well. Sin, introduce me at once to your companion. She sounds like a proper lady and dresses like one, too. Yet she stands rather close, and lets you touch her in public. I am *most* intrigued."

This was it.

Unclenching his jaw, Sin glanced at Grace. The tiniest nod indicated he continue. "Your royal highness. May I present the dowager Countess Carrington. Grace to her dearest friends."

The Prince Regent chortled, staring hungrily at her breasts. "Of course! No wonder Carrington kept you to himself. I would also. But the widow has come to town to let down her hair, hmmm? Naughty, naughty Grace. So, tell me. Exactly how well do you know our favorite Sin?"

"Rather well," she purred, shooting the prince a heavy-lidded look.

"One might say," said Sin, quelling the urge to punch the future king by lifting Grace's hand to his mouth and kissing each of her knuckles before deliberately curving his hand around her lush backside and squeezing. "We are very, *very* close friends. But do not tell Lord Baxter!"

"Oh indeed," added Grace quickly, "we beg you, sir, do not tell a soul. Lord Baxter is intent on courting me. Imagine if such an upright and morally sound man discovered I wasn't at all a virtuous widow!"

The prince's eyes gleamed. "Virtue is vastly overrated, my dear. But your scandalous little secret is safe with me. Now, I command you both to join me for champagne and sweets. Berry tarts, custards, cheesecake and whatnot, quite good I suppose, but not a patch on Fa…well, you know where."

Sin stifled a laugh. He hardly needed confirmation that Prinny was responsible for all the salacious gossip about Fallen's activities. The man leaked like a rusty bucket. But judging by the malicious smiles and flurry of movement in the royal box, not to mention the boxes on either side, his and Grace's *secret* was now moving at the speed of a runaway cart from *ton* member to *ton* member.

He'd estimated about an hour for the news to spread across London. It seemed that was entirely too conservative. Baxter would be hailed and informed and consoled by 'concerned friends' in half that time.

By tomorrow evening at most, Grace would be a free woman.

Who wouldn't need him any longer.

Fuck.

Chapter Five

Wincing as Nell arranged her hair into the ugliest, plainest, most no-nonsense coiled braid in the history of style, Grace worried her tender lower lip, the recipient of her anxiety for several hours now. "Stop looking at me like that. I hate it as much as you do."

Her maid harrumphed. "My eyes are merely encouraging you to tell me what on earth is going on. When your father and stepmother arrived in high dudgeon this morning, I thought for sure the Vauxhall outing had worked a treat and Baxter was no more. But now the four of you are attending a church roof fundraiser?"

"I don't understand it myself. The Prince Regent made such a fuss over us last night, and Sebastian—"

"Sebastian now, is it?" said Nell with raised eyebrows. "My, my."

"Oh hush up. Anyway, he told me half the Carlton House set were there and galloping the news to the four corners of the Gardens and beyond, so it is impossible for Lord Baxter not to have heard. I'm going to send Sebastian a note. Ask him to meet me at the fundraiser."

Nell nodded as she sank into an unhappy heap on Grace's bed. "I think that is a good idea. You may need a friend later, especially with the bishop and your stepmother firmly on the side of Lord Baxter."

Anger flared again, the foot-stomping, vase-hurling kind, and her fingers clenched around her small jewelry box. She'd asked for two weeks. Just fourteen nights on her own, and her father had again broken a sworn promise, bursting in with vile Edwina in tow. "No need to remind me. I just hope Sebastian doesn't have a prior engagement."

"Indeed. Oh, Lady C, although I truly hope the Vauxhall outing worked, I'm sad you never got to try out some other toys. Or see the pirate room…"

Grace's shoulders slumped. "You and me both."

Several hours later, she strolled into the parlor of a stately wood and stone London townhouse. Lord Baxter's grip on her elbow was more gaoler than fiancé. In her heeled slippers she was an inch taller than him, and despite the fact she wore a high-necked gray silk gown adorned with a single, discreet cameo, and her hair in the terrible bun, the wretched man had still tightened his lips and insisted she showed more flesh than appropriate for a respectable lady. Only already running late had prevented him imposing his preference for a complete change in clothing.

"Ah, Lord Baxter! You are most welcome," chirped a plump matron clad entirely and rather unfortunately in orange satin. "And who is this fetching…why, it's *Lady Carrington*. My dear, I'm so relieved to see you two together! Miles returned from his club late last night with the most frightful tale…but here you are, and his lordship in escort with all proper devotion. How wonderful!"

"Lady Miles," Lord Baxter chided coldly. "A refined female pays no heed to the idle gossip of curs and whores.

Your husband is most lax in his instruction."

Their hostess drooped. "You are right, my lord. I do beg your pardon. Oh, Lady Carrington, how fortunate you are to have gained the affection of a man such as Lord Baxter. So proper. So righteous. I enjoyed tremendously his most recent speech on the evils of lowborn women, the vulgar, shameless harlots who dare put pen to paper and call it writing, who shelter runaways and orphans, who put the world in disorder when they marry above their station. I was truly, truly inspired. Did you hear it?"

Grace swallowed hard, lest the scream building in her throat unleash itself. "Ah, no. No I have not, Lady Miles. May we sit anywhere in the parlor? I should like to find enough room for my father and stepmother also."

"Bishop Lloyd-Gates is here?" said Lady Miles with a gasp. "Oh gracious me. Gracious me! We are twice fortunate. I must share the good news. Do excuse me, and please, take the seats in the first or second row so I might point you all out. The committee will be in transports. Transports!"

As their hostess bustled away, Grace gritted her teeth and forced a smile upon her face. "I wonder how fundraising is progressing for the church roof."

Lord Baxter gave her a small but approving smile. "Very well. I'm going to present the committee with a draft for three hundred pounds this evening. That will take them over and above the remaining amount they needed to restore the building to its former glory."

"Most generous of you, my lord."

"Lady Carrington," he replied, his grip tightening further even as one thumb traced a brief circle on the soft skin of her upper arm. "Grace, if I may. I am a generous man. To a quiet, decorous, obedient wife, a true lady who knows her place and endures marital relations without complaint, I would be a very generous husband."

Nausea churned. "Oh. I, er—"

"Carrington's earldom was laughably new. His lineage weak, diluted with commoners. But our ancient bloodlines together will breed sons to own the country and clergy. Pretty daughters groomed for the palaces of England and Europe. Each time you were brought to childbed, I'd reward you with tasteful trinkets and jewelry. You'll have all a woman needs."

One more word and she was going to be violently ill.

"Please excuse me, my lord," she choked out, twisting her arm from his grasp and dipping into the shallowest of curtsys. "My stepmother is calling me over."

Fleeing at a near-sprint, uncaring who might see her or what they might think, Grace dashed across the room then veered left and left again down a series of narrow, dark paneled hallways. These houses built in the time of King Henry VIII might be problematic when it came to light and space and ceiling repairs, but they were altogether wonderful when it came to getting oneself thoroughly lost—

The thought dissolved in a stark flash of terror, as a large, strong hand wrapped around her arm and dragged her into a darkened alcove. Struggling against the iron grip, Grace's cry for help to rouse the entire city was reduced to nothing more than a muffled squeak when her captor's other hand clamped over her mouth.

"Shhh, it's me, darling," whispered Sebastian in a rough voice so welcome, she turned and burrowed against his chest in sheer relief. "I came as soon as I got your note. Is it over and done with? Are you free?"

"No," she said bitingly. "It seems Lord Baxter heard tales of my behavior from many sources last night, but chooses not to believe them as they come from the mouths of *curs* and *whores*."

"Damn his bloody priggish hide. Well, I guess we'll have to make it so he cannot help but see reason."

"How?"

Sebastian smiled at her, a slow, rakish grin that hardened her nipples and caused her clit to throb. "Why, a depraved spectacle right under his nose, of course. If we moved to a more suitable, easily discovered location, do you think you could moan and scream for me loud enough to shake the very foundations of the Miles's townhouse?"

"With you there is a strong likelihood of that," Grace replied with a shiver of anticipation as she went up on tiptoes to brush his mouth with hers, and rub her aching pussy against his cock. "And here you are, helping me again. I…you're the best of men."

"Gracie, it is my pleasure. In all ways."

...

On another occasion the Miles' townhouse would have been perfect for a secret tryst. The sheer number of alcoves, darkened hallways, and wide window ledges ensured enough possible locations to service an entire bloody regiment. Unfortunately, a place like this was a damned annoyance when you and your lover actually wanted to be found.

Growling in frustration, Sin turned away from yet another shadowed corner. "Too bloody private."

Grace glared at him. "Sebastian! At this rate we'll be back in the music room fucking while the church roof committee fundraises around us."

He stilled, unable to stifle a grin. "Did you just say *fucking*?"

"I, uh, well…I may have. So what if I did?" she replied defiantly, lifting her chin.

Giving in to the temptation to touch her, Sin cupped the back of her head with both hands and gently delved under the high neck of her appalling gown to stroke her soft skin with his thumbs. "You must know that when words like fucking and pussy and clit come out of your sweet, ladylike mouth, I get so hard it hurts."

"Indeed?" said Grace slowly, stepping closer and rubbing those taut little nipples against his chest again. "In that case… do you know I dreamed of you all night after I got home from the Gardens? My backside was still tender from the dildo, and my pussy and clit swollen from the way you took me so wonderfully hard and deep in the carriage. When I woke up wet this morning, I…I actually reached for you to ease the ache."

Sin stared at her heavy-lidded eyes and pink cheeks, speechless with lust. Again the unpleasant thought of how he would ever be able to say a final goodbye to this woman stormed into his mind, and it proved impossible to set aside.

Angry at his own weakness, hating Baxter even more than before, and all the nameless, faceless, suitable prospective husbands of Grace's future, he kissed her hungrily. He was probably bruising her soft lips with such brute force, but he was unable to stop, not when her arms twined about his neck and all he could hear were whimpers as she melted against him. Finally he picked her up and set her on a wide, cushioned window ledge, standing between her spread thighs and rucking up her gown.

"Grace…" he said hoarsely, his control hanging by a thread at the sight of her damp curls, the intoxicating spicy scent of her swollen, pink pussy.

"Don't talk. Hurry!"

"Demanding, imperious, woman," said Sin, a rusty laugh escaping as he sank two fingers into her drenched slit, her slickness audible as he twisted and stroked. "Hmmm. I'm not sure you are wet enough to take me yet. Should I suck your nipples? Rub your clit? Perhaps finger your tight little ass for a while?"

"Do not tease me, Sebastian St. John," Grace said fiercely, and before he could move, she leaned forward, tore the top button of his linen shirt and nipped his flesh with her teeth. "Fuck me. Like you mean it."

Christ.

Violently aroused by her unashamed need, so close to coming he could hardly see straight, Sin somehow managed to unfasten his trousers and free his engorged cock. Coating the head in her juices, he thrust several inches in then pulled back, setting up an uncompromising rhythm to the symphony of her ragged moans.

"That's it, darling. Louder. Let them all hear you."

"Harder. Please. Oh God, please, more."

"Like that?" he asked, plunging brutally deep, the question entirely unnecessary as her fingernails dug into his neck and she climaxed with a wild cry. Barely able to withdraw in time, shocked at the selfish, primitive urge to break his own rule and risk a pregnancy by spilling every drop of his seed inside her, he came all over her mound and inner thighs with a low roar.

"Sebastian? Is something wrong?"

He quickly shook his head. "No. I just seem to have lost the ability to think. And remain upright. Excuse me while I slide to the floor and become syllabub. Or in my case, Sinabub."

The rich sound of Grace's laughter warmed his heart, and he leaned forward, capturing her mouth with his own. The tender kiss couldn't be more opposite to their frenzied fucking, and at that moment he knew he was in far deeper trouble than he'd ever imagined.

"We need a handkerchief," she murmured, her head falling back to rest against the diamond window pane. "There is one in my reticule."

After swiftly cleaning them both up, Sin stuffed the

handkerchief into his pocket and tucked his cock back in his trousers, but didn't fasten them. Nor did he fully lower Grace's gown. "I think I hear footsteps. Fear not, Lady Carrington, we are soon to be discovered."

"Will you be thrown out of the townhouse?"

"Probably not *thrown*. I did bribe my way in by making a donation to the church roof fund. Never ceases to amaze me how fast the cold and righteous forget their scruples in exchange for a bank draft."

"What kind of sum?" she said, looking at him not with avarice, but mild curiosity.

He shrugged. "Two thousand pounds. I know the church they are repairing; it is an old and pretty building, with some kind and truly Christian parishioners."

"Two *thousand*! Baxter was preening over three hundred."

"He would. No doubt he'll make them get on their knees and grovel for every penny as well," Sin replied, his gaze narrowing. "I saw the two of you talking, and his grip on your arm. What else did he say?"

Grace's lips tightened, and he regretted the loss of her soft, sated smile. "That if I am a silent, docile china doll, who accepts his painful, perfunctory bedchamber visits, I will have the honor of birthing sons to carry on his line, and daughters to sell to the highest-ranked bidder. All while gaining a veritable tidal wave of tasteful jewelry, figurines, posies, and hair ribbons."

His gut twisted, and he enveloped her in his arms, smoothing a hand over her hair as much to soothe himself as her. "What lady could resist such a thoroughly tempting offer?"

She looked away, but not before he saw the sheen of tears in her eyes. "Once upon a time I did want a child. Badly. But the thought of him in my bed...of being trapped in a cold marriage again with someone I despise in every way, ruling me, lecturing and molding my sons and daughters, punishing us all for any perceived transgression… I can't do it. I simply canno—"

A truly ear-murdering wail interrupted her, and Sin glanced sideways to see the red-faced visage of their hostess, a small army of appropriately outraged guests trailing behind her. "Ah, Lady Miles," he teased. "What a becoming shade of pumpkin you are wearing. Contrasts perfectly with your tomato-esque cheeks."

"Not one more word, sirrah, you…you despicable bounder! I see my husband's tale was gospel truth. And Lady Carrington acting the slattern…the two of you treating my home like…like a brothel!"

"I wouldn't say *brothel*," said Grace, in a voice so sultry it made his spent cock throb.

"Nor I," he added. "That is overly harsh, Lady Miles, not a penny has changed hands. Although if you'd like to negotiate a share as bawd, do let me know."

Red became purple, and Sin's lips quirked in alarm. Today it might be indeed possible to definitively answer whether a human head could implode.

"Get out," screeched Lady Miles. "Get out, get out, get out!"

"Sebastian," said Grace, not even looking at the woman. "Would you escort me back to my father and stepmother?"

"Be my pleasure, angel," he replied, refastening his trousers, assisting her down from the window ledge and adjusting her gown.

Surely now they had achieved victory.
Surely.

• • •

The memory of Lady Miles's scarlet-faced caterwauling

would never cease to make her smile.

Mainly because after their false start last night, this could now be pinpointed as the day she managed to get rid of Lord Baxter forever. And again she'd been pleasured mindless by Sebastian. What he'd just done to and for her lifted her heart to the heavens, but she couldn't even look at him as they strolled arm in arm back to the parlor, not when her pussy was still damp and thrumming from the relentless thrusting of his thick cock.

Oh God, not just his cock. His mouth, his fingers…the heated words he whispered in her ear, the way he moved between sweetly gentle and deliciously rough at any given moment.

"Darling," his voice purred in her ear. "You're making me blush."

Grace blinked. "Excuse me?"

"The sheer lust on your face. Thinking about what I just did to you?"

"No," she mumbled, cheeks blazing.

"Pity. I am. Every time your hand caresses my sleeve, every time the air delivers me light wafts of your rose soap and wet cunt, I want to find a bed to spread you across. The way you scream and grip my fingers or cock when you come is really quite addictive."

"Stop it," Grace hissed, almost stumbling at his blunt, erotic words. "I can't focus when you talk like that, and I have one more audience with Lord Baxter to fulfill."

Sebastian sighed. "You're right. Plus, I'm hurting myself. Don't be alarmed if I walk a step behind you, but I find myself in sincere need of your voluminous skirts. Or perhaps a pelisse I could carry?"

Her gaze darted down without thought, and she shivered at the growing bulge straining against his trousers. Oh sweet heaven. She'd just had that inside her, been soaked with his warm, salty-sweet come, and he was ready for a second bout.

"Grace! Where *have* you been? Lord Baxter here was worried sick!"

The militant tone of her stepmother, Edwina, yanked her back to reality. Swallowing hard, Grace forced herself to meet both the woman's accusing glare and her fiancé's ice-cold gaze. But before she could even begin the tale, a furious splutter sounded behind her.

"Where has your stepdaughter been?" Lady Miles snapped, in high temper. "Oh, I'll tell you where she has been. Perched on a window ledge enjoying lecherous acts with *that man*!"

Gasps sounded from every corner of the parlor, but a quick glance around revealed almost as many looks of blatant envy, as shock or disgust. Sebastian's reputation did indeed precede him everywhere.

"Rather surprised to see you here, St. John," Lord Baxter eventually said, in a frigid tone. "Don't recall seeing your name on the guest list approved for this private gathering."

"It wasn't!" squeaked Lady Miles, clenching and unclenching her hands in the folds of her orange gown. "I swear!"

Sebastian shrugged. "I was a late responder. But as soon as I heard of the fundraiser, I simply couldn't ignore the need. And the ladies here were so very grateful for my arrival, poor pets."

"They are but women in need of far stricter guidance," said Lord Baxter easily, but his shoulders were rigid and his eyes practically spat loathing. "Dare we hope you might have followed my lead and dropped a few guineas into the fund? Or are you quite the cit now and channel all your resources back into, er, *trade*?"

Grace quivered as she attempted to smother a snort of laughter. Her wretched temporary fiancé no doubt considered that the worst insult possible, completely ignorant of Sebastian's skill and lifesaving generosity toward others.

"Oh no," said Sebastian, quirking an amused eyebrow at her before smiling equably at Lord Baxter. "I was pleased to donate. I can only hope two thousand pounds is enough to make a difference to that charming church and the good people who worship there. My mother was a part of the congregation for a time, and they were always so warm and welcoming to her…I say, Baxter. Are you all right? Forgive an indelicate observation, but you've gone a rather unbecoming shade of tomato. No, wait, aubergine. Now, where have I seen that phenomenon recently…hmmm."

Lady Miles shook her fist at him. "Why, you unconscionable reprobate—"

"A gentleman wouldn't make such an uncouth statement," snapped Lord Baxter. "Nor would he put his hands on another man's property. Step away from my fiancée."

Sebastian turned and grinned at her, one finger slowly tucking an errant blond curl behind her ear then trailing sensually along her jaw. "It is my experience that Lady Carrington very much enjoys my hands on her."

"No," Edwina moaned, cupping her pale cheeks. "Oh no. Grace, what have you done, you stupid, stupid girl?"

Taking a deep breath, strengthened by Sebastian's touch and presence, Grace looked her stepmother square in the eye, and smiled widely. "*Everything.*"

Lady Miles swooned. Edwina's face twisted and she flailed her arms in apoplectic rage. Sebastian began to laugh.

"'Tis true," he said, his amber eyes gleaming. "My darling Gracie is a most willing and adventurous minx. By the by, Baxter. I must chide the use of such an archaic term as *property*. Good God, man, next you'll be saying a lady must endure rather than enjoy the bedchamber."

Lady Miles gasped from where she sat on the floor, having

been revived by a friend waving a vial of hartshorn under her nose. "Lord St. John!"

"Be at ease, my lady," said Lord Baxter, bestowing a small smile on the fallen pumpkin. "St. John's upbringing was far more *casual* than ours and Lady Carrington's due to his mother's background. A common strumpet wasn't she, my lord?"

Sebastian's laugh was carefree, but his eyes were stormy. Grace shuffled closer, about ready to spit on Lord Baxter's champagne-polished boots.

"No," drawled Sebastian. "Cherished companion to a select few in the upper echelons of power. Then she met my father and happily retired. But I daresay you are right, my upbringing being different to yours. Several generations apart and all that. Now, Lady Carrington, I wonder if you are a trifle parched after this afternoon's exertions and excitements. May I fetch you a glass of punch?"

She nodded. "That would be lov—"

"No time," said Lord Baxter with a bland smile. "The speeches are about to start. St. John, I do believe you have outstayed your welcome and should depart with all haste. Come along, Grace my dear, Edwina, our seats are reserved next to the bishop's."

Before she could blink, her fiancé hooked his arm around hers and started dragging her toward the front of the room. When she glanced back, Sin still watched them, and from this distance he looked troubled, as though torn between several emotions. The same as she.

"My lord," she gritted out, turning back to Lord Baxter and shaking her head at the fanciful thoughts. "I don't believe we are going to miss anything. The committee hasn't set up yet."

"Oh, I know. But I wanted a word in private with you. Edwina, would you mind?"

As her stepmother fled, Grace's heart skipped a beat. Was this it, the moment she'd been wishing for—him crying off and setting her free?

"Yes, Lord Baxter?" she said softly, keeping her gaze on the ground so he wouldn't see her joy.

"You have acted with atrocious disregard for propriety this afternoon, Lady Carrington. Allowing a lowborn whelp like St. John to touch you. Insolence toward Lady Miles and your stepmother. Causing scenes in the middle of a fundraiser. All conduct grossly unbecoming my fiancée."

"And so?" said Grace, hardly daring to believe her good fortune. Tentatively she lifted her head, ready to be faced with revulsion and righteous anger as he formally ended their betrothal.

Instead, Lord Baxter's pale eyes were bright with feverish excitement. "You may not be aware, but everyone invited here today is utterly beholden to me. Over time I have collected their debts, loaned them money, provided introductions, and done them favors. But one misstep, and I will collect. I own them. Just as I will own you."

"What?" she said, confusion and stark horror almost robbing her of voice. The man wasn't just awful, he was actually evil.

"They know I will destroy each and every one of them... their families, livelihoods, and social standing...should one word spread of your shocking behavior. But now your true depraved and willful nature is revealed, I must answer the calling. You require a husband with a stern, resolute hand, one who is prepared to employ whatever correctional methods necessary to ensure you stay on the right path. I will be that man. And so, Lady Carrington—Grace—we must bring the wedding date forward."

Chapter Six

"Apologies for disturbing you, my lord, but you have an unexpected visitor. She says she needs to speak with you urgently."

Sin glanced up from his parlor desk, where he was attending to the last minute list of costume requirements for the evening's annual pirate ship fantasy extravaganza. The most anticipated event on Fallen's calendar, the extravaganza allowed club members to either take full part in the most extreme and uninhibited of role-play orgies, or indulge their voyeuristic tendencies and watch from comfortable tiered seating. It promised to be an intense sexual spectacle and a half, as things tended to be when Vice was in command.

"Diaz, I have told you repeatedly to call me Sin, like everyone else does."

The butler folded his meaty arms and scowled, turning an already intimidating visage into quite possibly the stuff of nightmares. "And I have responded repeatedly, *señor*, that no Castilian would accept such familiarity between employee and employer. I will not disgrace the memory of my family with such behavior."

"Irritable bastard. After tonight, I'm giving you two full days off with pay. Find a nice woman, or man, if that is your preference, and enjoy yourself."

"No thank you, my lord. I am more than content with my life and hours here."

Sin tilted his head and studied the bald man-mountain in front of him. "You know, Diaz, if I didn't know better I might say you stay close to Fallen for a reason other than job satisfaction. Perhaps you've found that nice woman or man already?"

Something like pain flared in the butler's eyes, but it was gone in an instant. "The visitor, my lord?"

"Who is it?"

"Lady Carrington."

Sin cursed and leapt to his feet. "For God's sake, man, you don't announce Grace, you escort her straight in. Even when unexpected. Understood?"

Pushing past the other man, Sin hurried toward the foyer, anticipation and dismay fizzing in his veins. He hadn't gotten the chance to speak to Grace after bloody Baxter dragged her away, and ten o'clock in the morning was very early to be paying an unscheduled call. Had she come to confirm victory and say a last goodbye? Or something else?

"Grace?" he called, rounding the corner at such pace his boot heels skidded on the marble floor.

"Sebastian," she said, and seconds later she hurled herself into his arms and buried her face in his shoulder.

Christ Almighty. She was *crying*.

"Darling?" he said in alarm, carefully scooping her up and carrying her back to his parlor. "Tell me what is wrong."

As they settled on the chaise, and he chafed her cold hands in his, Grace's tearstained face lifted to his. "T-tomorrow at eleven o'clock in the morning, I am to be m-married to Lord

Baxter."

"No!" he snarled, the words like a fierce jab to the stomach. "We fixed it…Lady Miles and her fucking awful friends saw…"

"Except it seems they all owe great sums of m-money and favors to Lord Baxter. He has them on the tightest of leashes, you should have seen their faces later. It was bizarre—like what we did never even happened! If anyone did say a word, I think he would destroy them in a heartbeat and not break a sweat."

Sin clenched his jaw. "Damn it, he would, too. Baxter has a habit of surrounding himself with weak people easily led and influenced, or those in desperate financial situations. Power is everything to him, that is why he hates and rarely spends time with those who have more. Did he say anything else?"

"That now my willful and d-depraved nature is revealed, I need stern, resolute correction. My blasted f-father and stepmother agreed, so the wedding isn't cancelled, but brought forward."

His hands tightened around Grace's. "Like hell you need correction. No. Not going to happen. No way are you getting shackled to that cane-happy bastard."

"Cane-happy?"

Unable to look at her as memories scraped him raw, Sin stared at the floor. "Baxter's correctional tool of choice. A long time ago he was engaged to a friend of mine. Sara. He hurt her. And one day she…she died. I'll never forgive him for what he did, nor will I stand back and let him crush your spirit. You are too…warm. Too alive. To never hear that wicked laugh, or see your eyes sparkle again…hell."

"Look at me."

She said the words quietly, he could pretend he hadn't heard them, at least until he got himself under control. At the present time his eyes burned and his chest felt like it was clamped in a fucking vice. But then Grace dislodged her hands from his and scrambled into his lap, her warm, soft hands cupping his cheeks and forcing him to meet her open, compassionate gaze as she gently kissed him.

"Don't," he said in a strangled tone as the burn grew worse, and his breath came in short, choppy pants.

Her lips brushed his ear. "Sara's death wasn't your fault."

"Of course it was my fucking fault. I took too fucking long to get there. A carriage. Who takes a carriage? I should have ridden. Changed horses and ridden the whole way. It wasn't that cold, just some rain. Because I was a fucking milksop, I was too late. He knew I hated him. And he smiled. He fucking smiled when he told me the news. If that happened to you, I couldn't…I couldn't b-bear it."

Horrified at the sound of his voice cracking, and his blurred vision, Sin attempted to wrench away. But instead she forced his head into the crook of her neck, stroking and smoothing his hair, and he shuddered as moisture dampened his skin and hers.

Exactly how long they sat like that, he couldn't say. But eventually Grace leaned back and looked at him, her eyes suspiciously bright. "It won't happen to me. We won't let it. I have the start of an idea, but I need your help."

"Yes," he said hoarsely. "Whatever it is."

"We were gossiped about at the Gardens, but did nothing truly shocking. We partially broke the rules at the fundraiser, but Baxter's cronies won't speak for fear of retribution. What if we shattered the rules…here at Fallen? Tonight?"

Sin sat up so fast he nearly sent Grace sprawling onto the floor. "Of course! It's our annual pirate ship extravaganza. The scandal sheets call it the most decadent and downright immoral event in England. To attend is risqué enough, but—"

"I could take part!" she exclaimed, her eyes shining with hope. "Except…how would they know it was me?"

He rubbed a hand over his face, hating the thing he was about to advocate. "If you weren't wearing a mask, everyone would know who you were. See you practically naked, being touched and fucked. And when I say everyone, I mean the most important men and women in the country, including Prinny. Do you know how many anonymous notes are delivered to the press in the early hours of the morning following one of our events? Hell, nowadays lads are employed to stay and sort and check them, because they know they'll sell ten times the copies if a Fallen scandal is included."

"That's it!" she said excitedly. "Lord Baxter would hate that beyond all. Especially if it were you with me."

"Wait. *Wait*. This is no small thing. Your reputation would be destroyed."

Grace chewed her lip, her face the portrait of grave consideration. "It would be, wouldn't it? Then I should like our…display…to be no half measure. A man is one matter, but surely making love to another lady is infinitely more scandalous."

Sin choked on a laugh. Minx. "You really are determined to experience that, aren't you? With a redhead, by chance?"

"Do you have red-haired ladies who are members?"

"As a matter of fact, we do. And a few of them love nothing more than devouring the wet pussy and swollen nipples of a beautiful woman. But fair is fair, you'd have to return the favor. Knowing all this, do you agree?"

"I do," she said with wide eyes and ruby red cheeks, but her reply was so quick and firm, he did laugh this time.

"Then our next task will be taking you to Madame Alice and fitting a costume."

Bloody hell. This crazy plan might actually have a chance.

. . .

She'd never seen anything like Madame Alice's.

Rather than being situated in the heart of Mayfair like most other modistes and milliners catering to the wealthy, the large red brick warehouse was tucked away in a bustling corner of Blackfriars.

But inside, it was a whole other world.

Bolts of fabric—satin, silk, cambric, linen, twill, muslin, and velvet—were arranged in hundreds of colored rows. Cards of Brussels lace, ribbons, silk flowers, semi-precious stones, and dyed feathers rested in large, glass-fronted cabinets. Bulky, fearsome-looking footmen with pistols tucked into their belts stood guard at regular intervals around the perimeter, while two dozen neatly dressed, smiling women chatted, measured, fitted, and showed fashion plates to well-heeled customers.

"Ah! My beloved Sin," called a very stout, silver-haired woman with a warm smile as she hurried toward them. "You need something else for the ball?"

"Hello again, Alice," said Sebastian, taking her hands and kissing each of the woman's apple cheeks. "I need a special favor."

"Anything for you."

"My very dear friend, Lady Carrington here, requires a pirate costume. Can you help?"

Madame Alice pursed her lips. "To whom do you think you are speaking to, young man?"

"The second mother who changed my small cloths, fed me strained pears, and ensured I was fashionably attired long before I knew what the words meant," said Sebastian with an audible sigh, and Grace couldn't muffle a giggle.

"That is correct. Now, my lady, let me look at you. Hmmm. Adequate posture, elegant neck, large breasts, ample hips… all hidden under the most ghastly and offensive sack ever seen in London. Who created that lilac monstrosity? Tell me at once!"

Grace tried not to flinch under the woman's furious gaze. "Er, I'm not sure, Madame Alice. My late husband ordered my clothing and it was delivered ready-made to the country."

"Bah. Well, dearie, you've come to the right place. I've been creating costumes for Fallen since it first opened its doors, and I'm going to sew you something spectacular. Now, tell me who you would like to be this evening."

"Be?" she replied, confused.

Sebastian grinned. "Indeed, darling. Is it your wish to attend as a bold pirate queen? An innocent princess taken captive? A siren or mermaid luring men to their ruin?"

"Ohhh. Then I want to be a princess from a foreign land. A woman forced across oceans for an unwanted political marriage to an evil tyrant, when the ship is attacked and she is stolen by a reckless and courageous pirate who falls in love at first sight and introduces her to all manner of lustful acts."

As Grace took a breath, silence rushed to greet her. But before she could flee in mortification, Sebastian began applauding. "Bravo! Single best costume story I've ever heard."

"Most certainly," said Madame Alice, her lips twitching. "That was marvelously specific. I think I know just the pattern. Now trot along, Sin, there are cheroots, decanters of brandy, and today's newspapers waiting in your usual spot."

"No. I believe I'll stay and supervise."

The modiste's eyebrows nearly flew into her hairline, but after a moment she nodded and beckoned Grace and Sebastian to follow her to a section of the warehouse separated out by a heavy black curtain.

"All right," Madame Alice said briskly. "Lady Carrington, let's get that insult of a gown off you. Good, good. Now, dearie, hop up onto that low stool and I will take some measurements. Sin, my boy, if you get in the way, I will stab you with a hat pin."

Sebastian looked up from where he now lay sprawled on a velvet chaise, and held up both hands in surrender. A gesture utterly undone by a wicked grin. "Wouldn't dream of it, Alice my sweet."

The older woman harrumphed, but her gaze was tender as she turned back to Grace with a thin length of measuring tape. "That man. Stole my heart on the day we met, and somehow I've never wanted it back."

Grace bit her lip before she blurted something foolish, like she knew the feeling. But she couldn't stop glancing in his direction, both wanting new garments to make his jaw drop, and wishing Madame Alice would give them some privacy so they could hold each other again like they had in his parlor.

Never had she felt so safe. So cared for. But at the same time, so needed and free to be herself rather than a bloodline or pretty face. Still though, she couldn't help yearning for more than this evening's plan—listening to a lunatic part of her mind that whispered another way to ensure Lord Baxter would never be her husband was for Sebastian to marry her himself.

"Ungrateful idiot," she muttered under her breath. Lord Sebastian St. John had done more for her than anyone on earth apart from Nell. Not to mention he'd made his thoughts on marriage very clear, even if he did care for her.

"Lady Carrington. Lady Carrington! Yoohoo!"

"I'm sorry," she said quickly to Madame Alice, heat scorching across her cheekbones. "You were saying?"

"I asked if you had a preference for cut. You know, anything you want to show off or keep hidden."

"Um, of course I bow to your expertise. But I need something outrageous that emphasizes my bust and legs. Like a corset but far more comfortable. And a train that swishes when I walk."

Madame Alice winked at her. "Well I never. You do have

plans for the evening, don't you dearie! Reminds me of all my wonderful years on the stage. Now, one last question. What color would you like your princess costume? Lavender and gray are banned as options."

Pure longing curled her toes as she thought of tearing up all her wretched mourning gowns for the gorgeous fabrics and colors in the warehouse. Ruby red? A golden buttercup yellow? Hunter green or chocolate brown?

"I'm not sure. Sebastian?"

"Sapphire blue to match your eyes. Satin bodice, silver trim and crystals," he said in a voice that brooked no argument. The modiste inclined her head and ducked under the curtain, her retreating footsteps echoing on the stone floor as she clapped her hands and yelled for several seamstresses.

"I haven't worn blue in forever," said Grace softly. "Carrington didn't like it."

"Criminal waste," replied Sebastian, getting up from the chaise and prowling around her like a hungry lion. "Can't wait to see you in something other than half-mourning, although I admit, naked will forever be my favorite."

"I must concur when it comes to you, my lord."

His eyes glittered, and she took a shaky breath as he slid one hand under her chemise and trailed his fingers along her inner thigh, higher and higher until he brushed her mound. "Tonight is so very far away."

As his fingers deftly circled her clit, Grace closed her eyes and moaned, unsure whether in ecstasy or despair. The evening didn't seem so far away at all, but surging toward her like a tidal wave. If the third attempt, by far the boldest and most wicked plan yet, succeeded, Sebastian's promise was finally fulfilled and their time together ended. If the plan failed, she became Lady Baxter.

Either way, she lost.

...

Returning to Fallen was like stepping into a tavern brawl.

As soon as he and Grace walked through the front door, laden down with boxes, string-wrapped parcels, and drawstring purses near to bursting with spare crystals, paste jewels, and ribbons for the harem, a swarm of frazzled honey bees descended upon them.

"Sin! Vice is being a right bastard and won't stop shouting."

"Sin! That new valet tried to steal tonight's apple tarts. Cook brained him with a bag of flour, and now the valet says he's goin' straight to the scandal sheets to complain."

"Sin! The four girls and footmen who play pranks on each other…well it got out of hand. Devil found in favor of the footmen, so the girls took him hostage. A list of demands got passed under the door, but they'll only talk to you."

Handing his and Grace's packages to Diaz and two other footmen, Sin took a deep breath. "Ladies. Ladies! Firstly, I'll speak to Vice, but do remember he is the public face of the evening, and he just wants it to run smoothly and successfully. Secondly, the valet's contract forbids him speaking to the press, and if he does he will find himself in all sorts of serious financial and legal trouble. Thirdly…where the hell is Devil trapped?"

"His office," piped up a young parlor maid. "Poor, sweet man did accounts all night and fell asleep at his desk again, so they tied him to his chair with their dressing gown sashes, gagged him with an empty money purse, and inked his whole face blue!"

"My word," said Grace in a solemn voice, although her eyes were twinkling. "They do mean business. What are their demands?"

"Not very smart things, ma'am. A unicorn to ride into the House of Lords. Cook's secret recipe for syllabub.

Embroidery thread that never tangles, and, er…oh, yes, a Viking broadsword."

"I see. Perhaps, Sebastian, I could try negotiating with Lord Grayson's captors while you talk to Lord Vissen?"

Sin blinked, hoping his jaw hitting the floor hadn't made too loud a crash. "You want to help?"

Grace frowned at him in a manner usually attributed to Alice. "Well of course I do. You cannot attend to everything at once, and I daresay there is much to be done before the extravaganza begins."

Warmth suffused him, right to the tips of his toes.

Curling an arm around Grace's waist, he pulled her close for a fierce kiss, tangling his tongue with hers, until she sighed and melted against him.

"Very well then," Sin eventually murmured in her ear, ignoring the symphony of applause, catcalls, and whistles going on behind him. "Until later, my captive princess."

She shivered, and he couldn't resist a nip of her lower lip, the urge to mark her overwhelming. Finally he let her go and left the foyer, deliberately not looking back lest he give in to the strong temptation of putting all staffing issues to one side, dragging Grace to a chamber, and fucking her until they both couldn't move.

A thought he'd had almost continuously since the day they met. Except it was far more than that now. Like when he'd shared the story about Sara and chosen to stay while Alice pinned and draped. He'd never done either with any woman, never wanted to, but with Grace it just felt right. Hell, everything with her felt right. On several occasions when he lay alone in his oversized bed, for he'd barely looked at another woman since meeting her, he found himself wondering what it might be like if Grace were curled up beside him. Not as his lover or mistress, but his wife.

Abruptly, double doors were flung open in front of him,

and Vice appeared like an apparition from the underworld.

"Sin, you lovesick bastard. If you can remember how to bloody think, I need your opinion on the improved pirate ship. Extra construction is done, just have to fit the last of it, and we're running out of time."

Alarmed, he flashed his longtime friend a soothing smile. Usually immaculately attired no matter what the occasion or exertion, today the burly Scot looked like he'd taken a leaf from Devil's ledger and slept under a bridge. His red hair hung loose from its queue, stubble darkened his jaw, his shirt and trousers were torn and coated with wood shavings, and his fiery temper clearly hung on by the thinnest of threads.

"Firstly," Sin replied, "go fuck yourself. My thought process remains superior and intact. Secondly, by all means show me your masterpiece."

Vice grunted and waved him into the ballroom.

Bloody hell.

One third of the room was tiered in wooden seats lined with black velvet and dotted with miniature tables for food and drinks. But the other two thirds had been transformed from the usual basic pirate ship to something out of a painting; the structure boasting soaring masts and rigs, a single painted railing, a large wooden wheel, numerous padded benches, two dangling iron cages, painted ceramic cannons, a silk Jolly Roger flag suspended from the stern, and the carved outline of a beautiful, naked woman decorated the bow.

"Well?" said Vice irritably, tapping his foot. "What do you think?"

Sin let out a low whistle. "I didn't think you could better last year's effort, but you have. And then some. It's magnificent."

"Had to hire dozens of extra laborers, but I wanted to make everything sturdier, especially the cages. They have to bear the weight of several people, nobody likes to be distracted by ominous creaking. Same for the masts. I added little knee pads so the pirate queen can use them for her floggings and whippings."

"And a role play captive," Sin said casually. "Say, a princess. Where might she be?"

"Depends on the circumstances," Vice replied, giving him an unsaid 'you stupid Sassenach' eye roll. "Is the delectable Lady Carrington for everyone to share, to sample, or just to be seen?"

Sin gritted his teeth. "Under no circumstances is she to be shared. Sampled yes, but only by me and the lady of her choice. Since a failed finishing school experiment, she's always wanted to try another woman, you see."

"Interesting," said Vice, clearly struggling to suppress a laugh. "So definitely to be seen then."

"Yes. By as many gossips as possible. I want the loosest tongues, say Prinny and co, seated closest to the pirate ship… for the moment Grace takes off her mask."

"Wait. *What*? Are you three sheets to the bloody wind? Nobody takes off their mask here. It's the golden rule. Complete anonymity, remember?"

Heaving a sigh, Sin rattled off the situation in the calmest, most non-emotional voice he could muster, a slight victory considering he felt anything but composed. "And that," he finished, "is why she cannot remain anonymous. Not tonight. Everyone has to know."

"Jesus," breathed Vice, rubbing an absent hand across his jaw as he slowly nodded in agreement. "Baxter and her father both need a damned good thrashing. Men like that give Englishmen a bad name."

Sin snorted. "But all Scots are perfect."

"That we are. Why don't I have Diaz draw up a one-off evening pass inviting Baxter to come and see the star attraction: his fiancée? He doesn't have to witness everything, perhaps just the grand finale."

"That is actually not a stupid idea. If the bastard explodes at the sight of all the ladies freely enjoying themselves, that will be a great load off my mind."

Vice clapped him on the shoulder. "Consider it done."

As he watched his friend walk back to the construction area and bark instructions at the laborers, Sin exhaled slowly. Just a few more hours and this whole godawful mess would be behind him and Grace.

Then they could have a quite different discussion—about the future.

Hell. Please let this work.

Chapter Seven

A stranger looked back at her from the full-length mirror. One maintaining the illusion of a woman stylish, confident, and thoroughly at ease with her near-naked body.

Tilting her head, Grace continued to study her princess self, thankful for the mind-calming privacy of the Fallen guest chamber. Madame Alice and her seamstresses had performed a miracle, creating something from a fairy tale in just a few hours. If fairy tales were downright hedonistic, that was.

A sapphire satin bodice studded with crystals and trimmed in silver lace stretched from her underarms to the tops of her thighs, the sewn-in stays cupping and shoving her breasts so high it appeared at any moment her nipples might pop free. Embroidered silver muslin cascaded from the hem of the bodice, but only around the back, leaving her legs scandalously bare and offering glimpses of her pussy when she walked. A small tiara and sapphire-studded combs swept her hair back from her face, but allowed it to tumble freely down her back.

All in all, she felt…

"Beautiful. Absolutely beautiful."

Grace spun around in a whirl of whisper-thin fabric to see Sebastian propped against the chamber doorframe. He wore an open-necked white linen shirt with a jewel-encrusted belt about his waist, old fashioned black breeches, and had one booted foot crossed over the other. But while his pose was casual, his expression could only be described as *carnal*.

Emboldened by the lusty appreciation, Grace strolled forward with a deliberate sway of her hips. A smile of delight curved her lips when his gaze rested on her breasts, but when it dropped lower and halted, she laughed. "Sir! How dare you enter the domain of a princess without invitation."

"I believe you already have some idea of what I might dare, your highness," he replied with a groan. "Fuck. That costume. Alice is too bloody skilled for her own good. It will be perfect though, for later. Especially if…"

When his voice trailed off, Grace's eyes narrowed. "Especially if what?"

"Especially if Baxter accepts the one-off invitation that Vice sent him, and turns up here apocalyptic with rage that his *property* dares to defy his orders in the very center of, now, what was it? Willful depravity."

Her lips quirked as she kissed his cheek. "Naughty man. One would think you'd do anything to see this plan work."

"I would do anything," Sebastian said quietly. "To ease your mind and ensure your happiness and liberty. So in time you might choose to be with me."

Grace stilled, her heart about to beat out of her chest. Did he mean…"In time? What about right now?"

"Very well. Then know that once this bloody night is behind us, I wish to have a long and frank discussion with you about, er, certain matters. Certain future matters. The two of us in the future, as in tomorrow onward…fuck. This is why Vice does all the fucking speeches."

"It sounded rather perfect to me," she said, giddy with sheer joy.

"Madam," he purred, and in one swift movement his hand was between her legs and cupping her pussy, leisurely grinding his palm against her. "Are you by chance amused by my remarkable lack of eloquence?"

"Ah…no," she moaned, tilting her hips to give him better access. "Never."

A moment later Sebastian maneuvered her against the silk-hung wall, dropped to his knees and leaned forward until his breath teased the tight blond thatch between her legs.

Grace sighed, her hips circling of their own volition in slow, blatant want.

"Good," he rasped, his thumbs massaging her outer labia. "Glad to hear it, darling. Now, spread your thighs wide and show me that pretty cunt. I'm afraid we cannot go downstairs until you've come in my mouth, for the perfect finishing touch to this enchanting costume is your pussy and inner thighs all wet and glistening, and a spicy perfume of needs well met."

Oh God.

As the tip of Sebastian's tongue flicked her clit, her head fell back against the wall, and she threaded her fingers through his hair in preparation of the sweet onslaught. He was utterly focused as he held her labia apart and licked her, his tongue a hot, relentless arrow of exquisite pleasure as it alternately lashed her clit and plunged into her pussy.

Gasping for breath, Grace writhed against his hot mouth. When her juices coated his tongue and chin, he penetrated her with two thick fingers, twisting and curling and rubbing them against a place that made her cry out with sheer bliss, helpless against a whirlwind of intoxicating sensation.

"Please, Sebastian," she begged, ready to agree to anything if he would just boost her over that last edge and make her come. "Please, now."

Instantly he wrapped his lips around her clit, the delicate suction contrasting so perfectly with the rough drive of his fingers that she climaxed, shuddering and jerking as waves of ecstasy buffeted her whole body.

"Mmmm," said Sebastian, leaning back on his boot heels and licking his lips, watching with a rather smug smile while she recovered her wits. "Much better. Now we're ready—"

Not even allowing him to finish the sentence, Grace shoved him. Off balance, he fell back onto a thick woven rug, and she scrambled on top of him, one knee falling on either side of his thighs as her backside pinned his legs to the floor.

"Not quite," she replied in a low, sultry voice. Somehow she managed to undo the front flap of his breeches without tearing off the buttons, freeing his hard cock into her waiting hands.

Lowering her head she took him into her mouth, sucking gently on the swelling head while lapping the sensitive underside with her tongue.

Sebastian groaned, and this time it was his hands cupping her head as he wordlessly pleaded for more. Greedily she took him deeper, sucking his length down her throat while she clenched and unclenched one hand around the thick base and cupped his seed-heavy balls.

"Gracie," he muttered, panting hard while his hips bucked with such violence she swayed on her precarious perch. "That feels good. So damned good, darling. Your mouth on my cock, your hands…going to make me come so hard…"

Sebastian climaxed with a guttural groan. Reveling in the earthy taste of him, she swallowed hard then slid his cock from her mouth, delicately lapping it clean before tucking it back under the breeches flap and refastening the buttons.

Smiling serenely into his sated, half-dazed eyes, Grace braced her hands on his solid chest, rose to her feet, and smoothed the creases from her costume. "Now, my lord. *Now* we are ready to join the party."

...

The ballroom was rapidly filling with a crush of London's best—well-dressed voyeurs choosing their spots on the tiered seating, male and female pirates and captives mingling on the wooden ship deck waiting for proceedings to start—but Sin only had eyes for one.

The luscious, masked princess in blue satin on his arm.

No other woman in the room held a candle to Grace. Certainly not the combination of down to earth sweetness, wit, a wide-eyed enthusiasm for sex, and breathtaking beauty. And the best part was, she had feelings for him. Only a woman who truly held a man in affection could smile at the most ridiculous, vaguest, bumbling declaration of intent ever spoken, then a short while later, own him so completely.

Christ, he'd pleasured her to get her in the right frame of mind for the evening; he'd never expected her to return the favor. But when she'd taken charge for the first time, straddling him on the guest chamber rug and performing the best cock suck of his life…even the thought of it made his breeches uncomfortably tight again.

"Sebastian," said Grace, tugging on his sleeve. "Look at the ship! How splendid. And everyone's costumes. Does Madame Alice make them all?"

"Yes. Most orders get placed months in advance, so it's a very, very lucrative evening for her and the girls. An enormous amount of work, but unlike other modistes, payment is expected promptly on delivery, and I calculate a financial bonus for the seamstresses involved into each bill. They'll get the equivalent of a year's rent, food, and clothing from one ball."

Her hand curled tighter around his arm and squeezed. "I love that. All the wonderful, practical ways you help. I bet your mama looks down from heaven with such pride. Your father, too."

A boulder lodged in his throat and he looked away.

"It will be ten years next month. I miss them a lot." The words tumbled out before he could stop them. "Mama was so much fun, kind and loving and thoroughly unconventional. Father told me he knew the day he met her that she was the woman for him. I always thought that fanciful. Unlikely. But now…"

"I would have loved to have met them. Tell them what a fine son they raised," said Grace, cupping his cheek, and he reluctantly turned back, unsettled again by the feelings of vulnerability and awkwardness. Not even being able to string a coherent fucking sentence together. Damned bloody poets and playwrights had a lot to answer for, implying that this love business was all so natural and easy.

"I'm sure they would have—"

"Ladies and Gentlemen, Pirates and Captives! Please take your seats and places, ball festivities will begin in a few minutes!"

Glancing over at the footman bellowing his message to all corners, Sin exhaled with a mixture of relief and irritation. "That is our call, Princess Grace. Does your mask feel secure enough?"

"Perhaps it could be a little tighter," she said, turning her head so he could swiftly retie the silken thread. "Lead on, my pirate. I do hope I've been allocated a very public place in front of all these lords and ladies."

"But of course," he replied, dropping a quick kiss on her shoulder before escorting her across the ballroom floor and up onto the wide deck.

With a blast of trumpet fanfare, Vice appeared out of a cabin. The viscount was dressed up to the hilt in black breeches and boots, a hunter-green velvet jacket, white open-neck shirt, and black tricorn hat. One eye was covered in a black satin patch, and his fingers damn near glowing with heavy gold, ruby, and emerald-set rings. He stood at the ship's helm then strolled the length of the deck, barking instructions to his crew, halting here and there to test a whip or fondle a cowering captive.

The audience cheered and applauded wildly, and Sin almost joined in. Nobody commanded attention like Vice, and the fearless exhibitionist was in his element here.

"You! Pirate Sin! Who do you offer for my amusement and plunder?"

Sin bowed deeply. In the most carrying voice he could muster, he replied, "She is called Princess Grace, my captain. From a land far across the sea."

"Grace, you say?" Vice bellowed to be heard over the murmurings of the crowd, stunned at the mention of a name. "Well, show me. Show us all the hidden treasure from such a land. She looks ripe for the taking!"

He glanced at Grace, and at her quick nod, he lifted her up onto one of the wide padded benches. Angling her so she mostly faced the now rapt crowd, he stood behind her, one hand cupping her right breast, while the other idly stroked her slick pussy. "Princess Grace is indeed ripe, my captain. Intended for the tyrant king of Baxterland, I stole her for my own pleasure and trained her in the ways of wickedness. What an apt pupil she turned out to be."

"I must see this. A demonstration?" called Vice, briefly meeting his gaze. Sin inclined his head, and Vice turned to the audience. "Who would see this once innocent princess mercilessly plundered?"

Cheers, applause, and whistles lifted the roof as Vice urged them on with further lewd suggestions and plans. Sin took the opportunity to talk to Grace, under the guise of kissing her neck. "All right, darling?"

"I'm eager. And nervous. And overwhelmed, all at once," she whispered, moaning softly when he pushed a finger into her pussy. "But I'd like to come again. With you inside me. Can we do that?"

His cock surged and he gritted his teeth. "Of course. But it can't be just you and I for the performance, we need another at least. Perhaps it is time to find your redhead."

She tensed, and he wanted to call the whole bloody thing off, bundle her in his arms and take her back to his own chamber. Then she tilted her head and looked up at him, licking her lips. "Yes please."

Nipping her neck, Sin laughed. "Wonderful minx. Captain! I put forward a plan for your consideration."

Vice turned, one eyebrow raised in interest. "Yes?"

"Princess Grace is headstrong and untamed. I believe she should be forced to endure the attentions of another woman as punishment for her wanton behavior."

Vice grinned, inclining his head to Grace, before turning and marching to the highest point of the deck where a large throne-like chair decorated with gems and oversized cushions waited. Sprawling across it, he picked up a silver bell, and rang it loudly.

"Here is my command. In the main entertainment of the evening, Princess Grace shall be fucked by Pirate Sin and a female captive of his choosing!"

The crowd roared their approval. Sin took a deep breath, but Grace turned her head again and nudged him. "Go on. I trust you, Sebastian."

He smiled. "Then let us begin."

...

If it weren't for Sebastian, Grace might have lost her nerve completely.

The crescendo of noise rising and falling around her, the sheer number of masked men and women watching, touching themselves and others was beyond comprehension. But he stood behind her like hewn stone, talking, caressing her breast and lightly fingering her pussy, both anchoring her and ensuring she remained on a knife edge of promised pleasure.

"Pirate Sin!" called Lord Vissen from his throne. "The female captives will now parade by. You may choose one to assist in Princess Grace's punishment at your leisure."

"As you wish, captain," said Sebastian. In her ear he whispered, "Any preferences?"

Grace's gaze roamed over the masked women on the deck. Tall and short, plump and slender, redheads, brunettes, blondes, and ebony-haired, all bound and half-naked. Most were pale, but a few of the women possessed the sun-kissed hue of Spain or Portugal. A dark-skinned lady with a beautiful smile, heavy breasts, and pointed nipples the color of blackberries almost made her change her mind, but in the end her long-held redhead fantasy won out.

"That redhead over there. The tall, slender one in the green breeches," she whispered back.

"You have exotic taste, darling. The lady is a thrice-married duchess, visiting from Prussia."

As soon as the duchess was brought forward, the rest of the captives knelt down on small cushions scattered across the deck. Other pirates ambled amongst the women, kissing them, fondling bared breasts, some tugging unbound hair or administering light blows with a riding crop, invoking audible sighs and whimpers.

Grace squirmed, a fresh trickle of moisture bathing Sebastian's fingers.

"Hurry, captive," he growled at the beautiful redhead as she scrambled onto the bench. "I grow tired waiting for you, when the princess must be punished at once."

"Beg pardon, my lord. I am yours to command," said the duchess in musical, heavily accented English. She stood before them, her head bowed in submission.

Sebastian delved into Grace's bodice and cupped her breasts, lifting both so her nipples were bared. "Suck the princess's nipples."

Looking up, her silver eyes visible through the mask and bright with anticipation, the duchess stepped forward. Soon Grace whimpered as the softest lips imaginable surrounded one swelling peak and gently drew on it, while a warm pink tongue flicked and lapped. So different to when Sebastian pleasured her nipples, and she missed his harder suction, the way his stubbled jaw stimulated her to further heights, but it still felt marvelous.

Abruptly Sebastian pushed the duchess's head away and ordered the woman to kneel. A moment later Grace's right foot was braced on the ship's railing, opening her wide, and that warm, pink tongue was licking her clit.

"Oh God," Grace moaned, writhing as delicious sensation built and built, but she couldn't escape it, not when Sebastian's hands on her breasts, his powerful body behind her, allowed no movement.

"More, captive," ordered Sebastian, as he stopped massaging and started pinching her tender nipples. "Shove that tongue deep in the princess's cunt. Yes, that's it. Again. Again! Good."

The duchess made a sobbing sound, and Grace glanced down in alarm, until she saw the ecstasy on the woman's face, the way she'd delved into the front flap of her breeches to stroke herself. Overcome, Grace orgasmed with an abandoned scream, the other woman's pleasure, that skilled tongue in her pussy, the rough pinches of her nipples, sending her over the edge.

Grace sagged against Sebastian. He nuzzled her neck then stilled.

"Baxter's here," he breathed in her ear. "Back row tiered seating, to the left. Only person not dressed for the occasion, and looking rather murderous."

"Do remember to give him a wave," she murmured back, as he nudged her forward until she balanced on her elbows and knees. Then he lifted the muslin fabric until it draped over her back, baring her bottom entirely.

"Now, captive," said Sebastian in the loudest, harshest voice she'd ever heard him use. "Lie down in front of the princess and spread your legs wide. She's going to return the favor."

It was the strangest thing in the world to have another woman's pussy so close, but fascinating, too. Carefully spreading the duchess's tight red curls and pale brown labia with her fingertips, Grace lowered her head and tentatively licked the silken wet flesh.

Sweet heaven. She tasted *good*.

Firming her tongue as best she could, Grace dragged it along the woman's slit, then pushed it inside her. The duchess's cried out as she writhed and ground her soaked pussy into Grace's face, coating her lips and chin with moisture. Pleased, she licked even harder.

A low growl was the only warning she had, as Sebastian gripped her hips and thrust his engorged cock all the way into her pussy. From this angle he felt even longer and thicker than usual, and as the momentum shoved her forward, forcing her tongue deeper into the duchess's spicy heat, Grace moaned at the bliss of pleasuring another while being so expertly plundered from behind. The duchess climaxed first, triggering another powerful orgasm for Grace. As delicious, endless spasms wracked her whole body and made her scream, Sebastian thrust brutally deep then pulled out, and she felt the warmth of his thick seed coat her lower back.

Exhausted and boneless, she wanted to curl up and rest. But now was the moment to free herself from an unwanted destiny forever. Taking Sebastian's outstretched hand, Grace rose to her feet and climbed up onto the first rung of the pirate ship railing, giving the audience a clear view of her sated smile and well-pleasured body.

Then she searched the crowd until she found Lord Baxter.

And tore off her mask.

Shocked gasps echoed around the ballroom, swiftly followed by the dull roar of confused, incredulous, and fascinated patrons as they grasped the rebellion of the act. Several hundred pairs of eyes stared in hunger, waiting, gleefully anticipating an angry melee the likes of which they'd never seen.

Instead, a man at the front got to his feet, lifting his mask for a moment to give her a wink. Prinny! "Jolly fine show, my dear Grace," the prince bellowed, applauding. "Jolly fine indeed!"

Seconds later the entire audience joined in, the clapping and cheering and whistling thunderous enough to shake the foundations of Fallen.

Laughing, she waved, then turned and kissed Sebastian fiercely on the mouth. "Thank you, my love," she said, nearly having to shout as the applause grew louder.

"Ladies and gentlemen, Grace Carrington!" called Lord Vissen, as he appeared beside her, curving a hand under her arm and assisting her down from the railing. "Now, the princess is going to briefly rest in my cabin, but she will be back to greet you later. Isn't she a talented, bold, and very wicked lady?"

The crowd roared, and she bobbed a quick curtsy before two footmen escorted her to a small, darkened cabin at the stern of the ship. Temporarily alone while she waited for Sebastian, she took a deep breath, wanting to twirl and shriek with disbelief at what she'd just done. And yet she had no regrets. Not one.

"Lady Carrington."

Grace froze, every tiny hair on the back of her neck rising

both at the words, and the cold hatred in the tone. Taking a deep breath, she turned around.

"Lord Baxter. How did you get in here?"

"It is madness out there," he said, his pale blue eyes fixed on her through his mask, and entire body still apart from a long jet and gold cane swinging from one hand. "And I did have to attend to a footman in the hallway. But here I am."

"To end our engagement? Excellent. About time."

As if she hadn't spoken, he gazed around the small room. "You know, I didn't believe Vissen's note at first. After my warning at the fundraiser, I felt sure you would conduct yourself in the manner I expect. Yet here you are, nearly naked, sticky with another man's leavings. And a woman's, for that matter. You enjoyed yourself out there."

"Every second," Grace spat, but regretted her lapse in calm when the cane whipped down in a lightning fast movement and sharp, burning pain flashed along her upper arm. "And every second in future I won't see you. There will be no marriage now, this tale will be told and retold across the country for days to come."

Lord Baxter smiled like a viper might, and before she could flee, a blow to the abdomen left her doubled over. "Indeed. While it grieves me to lose your bloodline and close connection to a duke and a bishop, my wife must be a madonna, not a whore. And you insulted me several times with your willful depravity, a slight I cannot allow. So we will take a little trip, you and I, and I will show you where whores belong."

"No!" she yelled, stumbling for the door. But he grabbed a handful of her hair, twisting her around, and vicious pain exploded across the side of her head.

Nauseating, suffocating darkness enveloped her, and she knew no more.

Chapter Eight

He was so damned proud of Grace.

They way she'd embraced her sensuality and tried a new experience. Well, not just tried it but participated fully in front of a crowd including bloody Baxter, took daring and courage. And the way she'd laughed her glorious laugh and bobbed an impudent curtsy afterward, not to mention that loving, rather possessive kiss on his mouth…fuck. Actually, of all people, he owed Prinny a brandy, too, for starting the applause.

Shaking his head, Sin rubbed a hand over his face and grinned as he was finally able to politely leave a group of captives. It would probably take a chisel to remove the expression. And more than a lifetime to stop wanting Grace. He liked women, always had, and it brought him a great deal of satisfaction to assist them. But what he felt for Grace went way beyond that. Damnation, he loved being inside her just for the connection. And rather than being indifferent or against the idea, the thought of someday making her belly swell with child, hell, it was exhilarating. No doubt about it, he was smitten. And not the temporary kind, but bloody well happily hooked forever like his father had been with his mother.

Another two giggling captives stepped into his path, but he directed them to another pirate and marched toward the makeshift cabin. They'd won—Baxter had slunk for the door after Vice escorted Grace away.

Ducking around a heavy black curtain, Sin blinked in the shadowy darkness. "Humblest apologies, darling, I was unavoidably detained…"

His voice trailed off. He was alone in the tiny room. Confusion turned to unease when he saw the discreet maid's door wide open instead of latched shut. But when his gaze dropped to the wooden floor, unease became terror.

A scrap of torn silver muslin. Two spots of blood. A temporary pass to Fallen.

"Fool," he spat, hating himself for being so damned stupid and cocky. Baxter was as cold and cunning as a sewer rat, not some idiot dandy. And now he had Grace.

With a bellow of rage, Sin shouldered his way through the maid's door and barreled down the hallway. The shattering of an urn and two vases registered faintly in his mind, but he didn't slow.

"Sin! What the bloody hell are you doing?"

Devil's voice was loud in his ear, and he clawed shirt and skin in an attempt to shove past him. "Not now," he snarled. "Baxter has Grace. He stole her…blood on the floor…I'm going to fucking kill him."

"Hell," said Devil, his expression horrified. "Baxter is… hell. Which way did they go?"

"I don't know. I'm going to look outside."

"All right. I'll fetch reinforcements. We'll get her back, Sin. I promise."

Bursting out the side entrance door, Sin looked left and right, searching frantically for any sign they had come this way. A sapphire blue slipper lying on the graveled path was his first clue. A groaning footman clutching his bleeding shoulder the second.

"Where did they go, lad?" he barked.

"The street. I saw your lady friend and she looked ill, all floppy and such, so I tried to stop them. Got in one punch, but the bugger stuck me with his cane tip! I'm sorry."

"Not your fault. Get inside and have that shoulder seen to, and tell them to bring around a carriage at once."

The footman bowed and staggered away. Sin sprinted down the lamp-lit path toward the street. Every scrape and chuff of his boots against the gravel made him wince, but he quickly reached the solid brick wall, flattened his back against the edge, then stole a glance around it.

Tonight the moon was his friend, and he clenched his fists in fury and relief at the sight of Baxter about thirty feet away, half-walking, half-dragging Grace toward a town carriage. About to chase after them, Sin stumbled when a heavy hand landed on his shoulder and spun him around.

"What the bloody hell is going on, Sin?" hissed a curt voice. "Where is Grace?"

The tall man wore a club-issued mask, but in the shadow of the wall Sin couldn't read its number. A pirate costume, tricorn hat, and wig didn't help with identification, either.

"Not your business, sir. Just go back inside," Sin snapped.

"Like hell it isn't." An outraged female appeared beside the man, also dressed as a pirate. "She's our niece!"

Sin choked on a cough when the pair ripped off their masks and hats: The powerful Duke and Duchess of Waverly. Though fury consumed shock when a glance over his shoulder proved Baxter had reached the carriage and opened the door. "She's over there, being abducted by that bastard. And you two are preventing me from rescuing her!"

The duke cursed, smacking his palm against the wall. "Come on."

The trio ran out onto the street. But even as they made good ground, Sin could only watch as Baxter shoved a limp Grace into the carriage, swung himself inside, and slammed the door shut. A whip crack echoed through the still night, and with a clatter of horse hooves and creak of lacquered wood, the carriage departed with gut-churning haste.

"No," screamed the duchess. "Grace!"

Before he could reply, the sweetest of sights arrived—Devil and Diaz atop Dev's latest investment, a curricle with the comfort of a carriage, but designed and shaped for speed and agility.

"Get in," yelled Dev, as the curricle came to a grinding halt. "What are we following?"

"Baxter's town carriage," said Sin, as he, the duke, and the duchess scrambled onto the leather seats. The curricle charged smoothly forward, the air cool as the conveyance had only a roof, no walls or door, but that was the least of his worries. They had to catch Baxter before he hurt Grace further. Had to.

"Right," said the duke. "Explain to me what the hell is going on. Why has Baxter taken Grace? Why would he think for a moment he could?"

Sin glared at the older man. "Don't you dare pretend ignorance. You are the head of the family and approved the fucking match. Christ. Carrington was a cold fool, but now you and Grace's goddamned father hand her over to someone ten times worse? Men like you should be horsewhipped."

"Grace and Lord Baxter?" gasped the duchess, gripping her husband's arm as they rounded a sharp corner at great pace. "Oh no. Charles would never sanction that."

"Damned right I wouldn't. Don't like the cut of his jib. Never have."

Sin scowled at the duo. "Are you trying to tell me you have no knowledge of the marriage your dear brother the bishop is forcing on Grace tomorrow at eleven o'clock?"

Waverly grimaced. "What Harold says and the truth is not necessarily the same thing. How could we know when we've been in bloody Vienna for the past two months? Only got back yesterday, because Anne informed me if we missed the pirate ball my life wouldn't be worth a farthing. Hell and damnation. My brother has gone too far this time. And as for that bounder Baxter—"

All three groaned as the curricle jerked left, then right, one wheel lifting almost completely off the street as they raced around a slow-moving cart loaded with barrels of ale.

"No. He's mine to deal with," said Sin, trying to ignore his roiling gut as he stared defiantly at two pillars of society. Even if they did enjoy the odd naked pirate orgy. "I adore Grace, and if she'll have me I'm going to marry her."

Duchess Anne patted his knee and murmured "lovely" before swiftly pressing her fingers to her mouth. Clearly her stomach was enjoying the journey as much as his.

"I know you're of decent stock," said Waverly. "Your father and mother were both good people. Financials?"

Sin almost smiled. "No debt, substantial incomes from Fallen and various estates, also a few shipping interests."

"And you'll treat her and any children well?"

"Always. I swear."

"Good," said the duke grimly, as he gestured ahead of them. "Here's the chance to prove yourself."

...

Pain. Bad pain. And the world wouldn't stop swaying and jolting.

Inching open one eyelid, Grace struggled to get her bearings. She was lying down, and her head, stomach, and arm throbbed. But why did she feel so ill and dizzy? Groggily, she peered around the gloomy, lamp-lit space. It was still night, that much was clear.

"You are in my carriage, Lady Carrington."

"Baxter," she hissed, bracing one arm on the window as she swung her legs down into a sitting position. The movement caused her head to pound, and for one awful moment her stomach threatened to erupt at the sight of the revolting man sitting across from her. "What have you done?"

"Foolish woman. You had the opportunity to become my wife. To create a dynasty and know true power. But you are weak. Tainted. Just like the rest of them."

"You're mad," she said, not bothering to hide her contempt.

"I am not!" he barked.

"Bedlamite."

"Silence, whore! We'll be in the Rookeries soon enough. You like to be taken with an audience, well those vermin criminals won't hesitate, and I will enjoy watching them bite and tear as they break you with the punishment you deserve. You'll be sorry for crossing me. And St. John loses again… damnation, what now?"

Grace stilled, hope surging as the carriage hit several bumps then slowed to a crawl, and Lord Baxter frantically rubbed his hand over the fogged window to discover the reason. If she could just get to the door and lift the latch, she could hurl herself out. Anything was better than this madman's plan.

"Ohhhh," she groaned, shuddering as she slid closer to the side of the carriage. "I'm going to be sick."

"Don't you dare."

"So very sick," Grace repeated, throwing herself at the door, her fingers scrabbling for the latch. Nearly there…

"No!" screamed Baxter, grabbing her arm in a cruel grip and yanking her toward him, before jamming his cane hard against her throat and making her cough.

"Sebastian will kill you," she choked out, her arms flailing as she tried to ease the pressure.

He chuckled. "Stupid whore. St. John has never bested me. I enjoyed breaking his spirited little Sara, but I will enjoy breaking you far more. Even the thought of your cleansing, that creamy skin bloody and welted and bruised—"

The carriage hit another stomach-churning bump, lurched to one side and came to a grinding halt. On the floor and gasping for breath, Grace glanced out the window, but the shabby wooden houses, unpruned trees, and damaged cobblestones could have been anywhere.

A fist pounded on the outside of the carriage.

"Get out," said a muffled male voice. "We have your driver. And four pistols trained on you. We have no desire to dismantle your carriage, but will do so if need be."

Lord Baxter's eyes gleamed. "Or," he called back, "I could kill Lady Carrington right now."

Glass shattered, and a cocked pistol appeared where the side window had been. "You were asked nicely. Now I'm going to put a bullet in you for each minute you delay further."

Almost sobbing at the achingly familiar voice, Grace reached back for the door latch. "Sebastian! I'm here!"

Before she could push the door open, Lord Baxter's hand encircled her wrist, and his cane made a swishing sound as the blade extended.

"We are going to exit the carriage, Lady Carrington, but in a very orderly manner. If you attempt to run again, or fight me, I will bury this blade in your back. Do you understand?"

"Y-yes."

"Good," he replied, nudging the door open with his foot, twisting her arm painfully high behind her back, and prodding her forward.

Hardly daring to breathe, Grace eased out of the carriage,

the night air icy on her bare skin. The whole time she could feel Lord Baxter's breath on her neck, and the tip of the cane blade nicking her shoulder, the combination making her want to vomit.

"Grace. You have bruises," said another familiar male voice to her right, and she sagged in relief.

"I'm all right, Uncle. Just…don't do anything rash."

"Waverly," snapped Lord Baxter. "What the devil are you wearing?"

"I would have thought that quite obvious. A pirate costume."

"No. *No*. Your bloodline…your brother is a bishop!"

"My brother is a damned fool to be in cohorts with you. Do not think for a moment I will allow a marriage between you and my niece to go ahead."

Lord Baxter shook with rage, and Grace winced as the blade pricked her skin in two more places. "I don't want to wed this trollop anymore. But she must be punished for her indiscretions!"

As loud as fireworks, two pistols discharged. Lord Baxter let out a bloodcurdling yelp, and all at once her arm was free, and the pressure of the blade gone. Instead, the man was a deadweight against her back, and she twisted sideways so he fell to the ground, two separate bullet holes decorating the shoulder of his pale gray jacket. Seconds later Diaz and Lord Grayson were on either side of Baxter, roughly binding his wrists and knees with rope.

Her legs buckled, but Sebastian's strong, warm arms closed around her, lifting and cradling her against his massive chest. "Grace. I thought…I thought I'd lost you. Hell, your temple, your cheek…shoulder shots weren't enough. I am going to kill him."

"No, I am," said her uncle, scowling fiercely at Lord Baxter's inert body.

"Both incorrect," said a stern female voice. "I will end the rotten bastard's existence."

Grace blinked in shock, grateful for Sebastian's strength as the combined sickening throb of her head, cheekbone, stomach, and shoulder made her dizzy. "Aunt Anne, why are you here…dressed as a pirate?"

"Same reason you are dressed as a captive, young lady. Or should I say, Princess Grace."

Hot color flooded her cheeks. Oh God. Her own aunt and uncle had been at the club! "I, ah, um…are you well?"

Anne Lloyd-Gates grinned. "Remarkably so. Your uncle and I wish to apologize, though. We've been away in Vienna on diplomatic business the last few months and only collected our correspondence this morning. Otherwise we would have put a stop to all this Baxter nonsense long ago."

"Do you often attend the pirate ball?"

Her uncle laughed. "Every one, my dear. Good for a marriage to have some spice, even after thirty-five years."

Icy cold, sore, and struck with an attack of uncontrollable mirth, Grace buried her face in Sebastian's shoulder.

"Take me away, please," she choked out.

"Where do you want to go?" said Sebastian. "Your father's house?"

"No. I want to go home. To Fallen."

"Now wait one damned minute," said Waverly. "What fustian is this? You'll come and stay with your aunt and I. Unless of course there is a stronger claim. Say, a betrothal approved by the head of the family to a titled man of the right age, with a large fortune, good lineage, decent address…"

"Subtle, very subtle, your grace," said Sebastian, but there was amusement in his voice. "You couldn't have at least given me a minute? Or allowed travel to a more suitable location?"

"Pah. No time like the present, m'boy. I proposed to Anne as she sat in the middle of a mud puddle her mare had just deposited her into."

"Ha. I should've said no," said her aunt. "Shocking rake that you were. But Sin, my husband does have a point. If there is something you would like to say…"

Grace stilled, the pain and cold fading as joy dawned. "Sebastian?"

He took an audible breath. "I know I'm not the man you were dreaming of, someone in business."

"Yes."

"One third owner of a pleasure club and inclined to freeing women from pimps and bawds."

"Yes," she said dreamily, wishing he'd shut up and kiss her.

"Someone who deals with flour bag assaults, come-stained costumes, and chronic sweet shortages."

"*Yes*."

"A man known to the world as Sin."

Grace sighed. "You'll always be Sebastian to *me*, but how many blasted times must I say yes to your proposal?"

He froze in the starlit darkness. "You're accepting?"

"That's what I heard," said her aunt cheerfully.

"She said yes three times, you treacle-brained idiot," called Lord Grayson, as he and Diaz dragged Baxter back to his own carriage and shoved him roughly inside. "Now can we get the hell out of this unsavory corner of London before we're all murdered? I have ledgers to tally."

Grace threaded her fingers through Sebastian's hair and tugged his face down for a kiss. "Just to confirm, I love you madly and my answer is yes, Lord St. John."

For what lady wouldn't, when offered heaven?

• • •

Two weeks later

"Sin, as I have told you on five previous occasions, you are not going in there. It's bad luck to see the bride in her wedding gown before the ceremony. You'll see it on that day, and not a moment before."

He smiled his best choir-boy grin. "Come on, Nell. I haven't seen her since this morning thanks to Alice's army of seamstresses. At least give me some hints. Color? Fabric?"

"No," said Grace's maid-companion, folding her arms and giving him a stern governess glare. The woman had taken to Fallen like a duck to water, and now practically ran the place, which was both a good and bloody annoying thing. Like now, for instance.

"I'll pay you for information. Name your price."

"No."

He tilted his head, as inspiration struck. "I'll hold a mini-ball. Bet there are more than a few gentlemen who would line up to be disciplined by the indomitable Pirate Queen Nell."

The door swung open.

Whistling a cheery tune, Sin strolled into the guest chamber that Alice had commandeered as a fitting room for Grace's wedding finery. But to his vast disappointment, his fiancée sat alone at a baroque dressing table, wearing a quilted satin robe and brushing her hair.

"I thought you were having a fitting done."

Grace smiled. "I was. But Nell's instructions were, as always, to keep you talking until we could put everything away. You'll see my gown next week when we wed, and that is that."

"Damnation! She foxed me again."

"Dear, dear. What did entrance cost you this time?"

Sin scowled. "A mini ball. Her as pirate queen. You know, I'm convinced there is a ferocious dominatrix lurking under her motherly exterior. Vice might well have some competition for overseer of the pirate extravaganza."

She burst out laughing. "Possibly. But Nell certainly has

you pegged, my love."

"Hmmm," he murmured, lifting Grace off the padded stool and carrying her over to a chaise. "Would you be making jokes at your lord's expense?"

"Ah, perhaps," she said breathlessly, straddling his legs. "What might happen if I was?"

He didn't reply, just kissed her fiercely, pouring his whole self into the embrace. Tearing off her dressing gown, he cupped her right breast, massaging and stroking it, while his thumb tormented her nipple and made her whimper and writhe in his lap.

Yet soon she had him equally mindless, as she reached down and cupped his cock, squeezing and rubbing it through his trousers until he thought he might explode.

"Fuck," he snarled, as his hips jerked in desperate want and pre-come dampened the fabric.

"Oh God, Sebastian," she choked out, arching her back when he glided two fingers along her soaked slit and pushed them deep into her pussy. "Please, I need you inside me."

Sin *tsked*. "Gracie, Gracie, Gracie. Have you learned nothing? What did I tell you that first day in my parlor about being specific?"

Leaning forward, she put her lips to his ear. "I do beg your pardon for my shocking lapse. Very well, my lord, I want you to take that big, hard cock of yours and bury it deep in my cunt. I want you to put a finger in my ass, and when I scream, when I come so hard that my pussy grips you like a hot fist, I want you to stay inside and fill me with so much seed that I cannot help but become pregnant with your child. Is that specific enough for you?"

Christ.

"Yes," he said hoarsely, so mindless with need he literally tore his trousers to free his engorged cock. "Take it. Take all of me, darling."

Grace went up on her knees, took his cock in her hand, and fitted it to the entrance of her pussy. Then with a low, sultry moan, she slowly sank down, her wet pussy swallowing every inch of his cock until he was buried balls deep. "I will. And I do."

Up and down she moved, grinding her clit against his groin. He slid one hand around and cupped her backside, teasing the rosebud of her anus with the pad of one finger before penetrating her to the first knuckle.

Grace bucked, her cry of pleasure echoing in the room, her inner muscles dancing along the length of his cock and making him groan. Faster she bore down and harder he thrust upward while finger-fucking her ass, his other hand reaching up to wind her loose blond curls around it and tug, arching her farther so he could suck her nipples as well.

Abruptly she threw back her head and screamed, her cunt gripping him and pulsing so intensely he thrust brutally deep and came, his seed pouring inside her welcoming warmth in long, excruciatingly good spasms that lasted and lasted.

Gasping for breath, he moved the hand in her hair to stroke her jaw, then leaned forward and kissed her, a light brushing of her swollen lips. "I'll be rather disappointed if that doesn't result in a baby."

"I think," she said, resting her forehead against his, "that we should probably do this often, just to be sure of success."

"You're clearly gifted. Gracie the genius, my delicious wife to be. You know, darling, I almost feel like we should send Baxter a gift for bringing us together. Perhaps some flowers. Or a decanter of brandy."

"Don't be ridiculous, Sebastian. Trinkets. A cartload of the cheap and cheerful ones to brighten his sickbed. Or perhaps his own pirate captive costume? He would love that."

"Minx."

"Indeed," she said, cuddling closer. "And don't you forget

it."

Leaning back on the chaise, he gently stroked her back. As if he could forget the way this witty, beautiful, seductive, tender-hearted, bishop's daughter had appeared in his life and staked a permanent claim on his heart. Every day of marriage to her would be an adventure.

And damn it, he couldn't wait to begin.

Acknowledgments

A special thank you to the members of the RWA Beau Monde chapter. Your collective Regency wisdom and ready assistance is greatly appreciated.

About the Author

Nicola Davidson worked for many years in communications and marketing as well as television and print journalism, but hasn't looked back since she decided writing wicked historical romance was infinitely more fun. When not chained to a computer she can be found ambling along one of New Zealand's beautiful beaches, cheering on the champion All Blacks rugby team, history geeking on the internet, or daydreaming. If this includes chocolate—even better!

Keep up with Nicola's news on Twitter, Facebook, or her website www.nicola-davidson.com

If you love erotica, one-click these hot Scorched releases...

ONLY FOR YOU
a *Lick* novella by Naima Simone

It's been five years since Gabriella James damn near destroyed me with her betrayal, sending me to hell in a cage. I've crawled free and continue to battle my demons through underground fighting and sex. But now Gabriella's back, begging for forgiveness. All I want is what she's denied me for all these years—her body. I don't trust her, and I'll never forgive her. But that won't stop me from taking her. Over and Over...

BREAKING HIM
a novel by Sherilee Gray

Folks in town say he's dangerous. But I know him as Elijah Hays, the quiet, gentle giant who works with the horses on my ranch. I feel him watching me, making me burn in a way that both frightens and thrills me. All I can think about is exposing the dark desire I see deep inside him—that low, gritty voice rasping orders in my ear, those huge, rough hands holding me down. I want his surrender, his control. I want to break him...and have him break me...

Hands On
Part One of the *Hands On* serial by Cathryn Fox

When hot as hell Danielle Lang showed up and asked me to teach her about sex, I thought I was hallucinating. Turns out the beautiful psychologist needed an extra bit of schooling in all things sexual so she could teach a class. I've got a football career to get back to. And she doesn't want to be a part of my world. There's no way we can be together—so I'm going to make sure I enjoy every sexy second…

Shameless
a *Playboys in Love* novel by Gina L. Maxwell

People say I'm shameless. They're right. I like my sex dirty. It takes a hell of a lot to tilt my moral compass, and I always follow when it's pointing at something I want. Especially when it points straight at the one girl in all of Chicago who's not dying for a piece of me. She's all I can think about, and that's a problem, because she wants nothing to do with me. But I've seen her deepest secrets, her darkest fantasies. Now I just need to show her how good it can feel…to be shameless.

Also by Nicola Davidson

HIS FORBIDDEN LADY

ONE FORBIDDEN KNIGHT

Made in the USA
Charleston, SC
19 November 2016